"The South of France—this is so exciting!"

Jack had to agree with Lily.

Exciting...but damned inconvenient that his libido had come roaring back after being nonexistent for so long. And he'd just promised to take the sexiest woman he'd ever met to the most romantic place on earth—and treat her as a sister.

Lovely. Lovely Lily, with sparkling green eyes and glossy peach lips begging for him to kiss them. For him to pull her into his lap and show her what real French kissing was about. But...no.

"When do we leave?"

"If we take the high-speed train, we can leave early tomorrow and be in Avignon in under four hours."

"Only four hours," she breathed. "I won't get a wink of sleep tonight."

Jack gave her a dry smile.

Neither would he...but for a much different reason.

Dear Reader,

I have been in love with the South of France ever since college, when I minored in French. As part of a class, I watched the classic film *Jean de Florette* and its sequel, *Manon des Sources.* These two sad but epic films were set in Provence, and the land itself seemed mysterious—tough and dry, but able to produce flowers of such beauty, especially the famous lavender prized around the world for its healing qualities.

Provence seems like a place that would help people heal, as well. In *Royally Seduced,* the second book in my royal wedding trilogy, Jacques Montford, the Count of Brissard, and travel writer Lily Adams are both in need of some tender loving care when they meet in Paris. Jack, a disaster-relief physician, is recovering from an illness that almost took his own life as he was trying to help others. Lily wants to explore as much of France as she can. She grew up the poor girl in a rich neighborhood and has not traveled in Europe like her classmates did.

Jack impulsively invites her to his lavender farm in Provence. When Lily accepts, they set out on an adventure at the height of the lavender harvest.

Their passion blossoms under the sun, but will it grow into love or fade away after summer?

A couple of fun notes about lavender—it has been in use for at least 2,500 years. The Romans may have named it after the Latin word "lavare," meaning "to wash." It also has aphrodisiac qualities—legend says Cleopatra used its perfume to seduce both Mark Antony and Julius Caesar. If those two powerful men fell under its spell, think what it can do for the rest of us!

Happy reading!

Marie Donovan

P.S. Visit my website, www.mariedonovan.com, and the Blaze Authors website, www.blazeauthors.com.

Marie Donovan

ROYALLY SEDUCED

Harlequin®

TORONTO NEW YORK LONDON
AMSTERDAM PARIS SYDNEY HAMBURG
STOCKHOLM ATHENS TOKYO MILAN MADRID
PRAGUE WARSAW BUDAPEST AUCKLAND

Recycling programs
for this product may
not exist in your area.

ISBN-13: 978-0-373-79648-9

ROYALLY SEDUCED

Copyright © 2011 by Marie Donovan

www.Harlequin.com

Printed in U.S.A.

ABOUT THE AUTHOR

Marie Donovan is a Chicago-area native who got her fill of tragedies and unhappy endings by majoring in opera/vocal performance and Spanish literature. As an antidote to all that gloom, she read romance novels voraciously throughout college and graduate school.

Donovan worked for a large suburban public library for ten years as both a cataloguer and a bilingual Spanish story-time presenter. She graduated magna cum laude with two bachelor's degrees from a Midwestern liberal arts university and speaks six languages. She enjoys reading, gardening and yoga.

Please visit the author's website at www.mariedonovan.com.

Books by Marie Donovan

HARLEQUIN BLAZE

204—HER BODY OF WORK
302—HER BOOK OF PLEASURE
371—BARE NECESSITIES
403—SEX BY THE NUMBERS
470—MY SEXY GREEK SUMMER
493—HER LAST LINE OF DEFENSE
530—KNOWING THE SCORE
638—ROYALLY ROMANCED*

*A Real Prince

To my own Eleanor of Aquitaine.
A sunny French book for a sunny girl.
With much love always.

1

LILY ADAMS STOOD in front of her New Jersey apartment building shivering in the predawn morning skies. Although it was July, the air was still damp and chilly at four in the morning. Her cousin Sarah and her cousin's husband Curt should be here any minute to take her and Sarah to the airport. She and Sarah were less than a year apart in age. Sarah's dad was the brother of Lily's late father, and he had done his best to act as a stand-in dad. Although Lily and Sarah had grown up in different suburbs of Philadelphia and gone to different schools and colleges, they had gone to summer camp together and shared major milestones.

And now they were sharing a fabulous trip together. Lily shivered again, this time in anticipation. Her first time in Europe! Sarah had studied in France and was a high-school French teacher, but Lily was a total newbie. A European newbie, so to speak.

After graduating from college with a somewhat-less-than-lucrative journalism degree with an even-less-lucrative English-literature minor, Lily had decided to remedy a childhood of never going anywhere by starting a modest career as a travel writer. So far, she had done several articles on her native city of Philly and had branched out to New Jersey and New York.

But writing articles for the local parenting magazine on top ten historic sites for kids in Philly was shooting fish in a barrel. Adventure lay outside the Tri-State area, so she'd scraped together enough money for a trip to France. Just her and Sarah for the next few weeks.

She craned her neck. Yes, that was their car, a dark sedan that glided smoothly to the curb. Sarah hopped out… in her pajamas? Comfort was important for flying, but, well, okay. Lily didn't much care what their fellow passengers thought of her cousin's baggy pink T-shirt and red flannel pants, complete with monkeys dangling off palm trees. It was all good, as long as Sarah could pass through security without being tagged for crazy.

But Sarah also looked like death warmed over, her short brown bob scraped back by a linty black headband that looked like an Alice in Wonderland reject. Her face was pale even in the dim light, and her lips were dry and cracked.

"Um, are you okay?" Stomach flu on an international flight would be kind of dicey.

Sarah's mouth spread into a wide grin and then she burst into tears of all things, clutching Lily as she sobbed. Curt hopped out of his side of the car and hurried to them. "What the heck is going on, Curt?"

"No!" Sarah jerked her head up, her expression alarmingly close to a snarl. "Don't you dare say a word!"

Curt and Lily cringed. "Of course not, darling. It's yours to tell, precious." He wrapped his arm around his wife's shoulder and kissed the top of her limp hair.

Darling? Precious? Curt was usually about as romantic as a rock.

"Sarah?" Lily said cautiously. She wasn't sure what was

going on, but she had a nonrefundable ticket to Paris leaving in about four hours.

Her cousin's face smoothed out until it was almost beatific. "Lily, I'm pregnant!"

Lily shrieked loud enough to wake the neighbors, who wouldn't bother calling the cops even if it were some mad strangler coming into her apartment. "Pregnant!" She started to jump up and down but quickly stopped when she saw the queasy look on Sarah's face.

"I know, I know! After all these years, all those times when it didn't work out…"

Lily gave her a quick kiss, remembering Sarah's several miscarriages until the damn doctors had figured out she'd had a blood clotting disorder all along. This trip to Europe was supposed to be a kind of decompression from the pain and stress of her infertility and losses—no pressure to conceive with a husband five thousand miles away. "But how did you find out?"

Sarah giggled. "I'd been feeling kind of off for the past week but I figured it was a touch of flu. Then last night about eight, I started throwing up hard, and Curt was worried. He took me to the E.R. They put in an IV but also ran a pregnancy test." She shrugged, her face splitting into a grin. "And here we are."

"Well, of course you can't go." Lily wouldn't have her cousin risk her baby on a strenuous overseas trip.

Curt's shoulders sagged in relief. He had obviously expected some hassle.

"But, Lily, how will you manage all by yourself? You don't speak a lick of French, and you've never been anywhere."

Great for her self-confidence. "Didn't you tell me that if you ever got pregnant again you would need very close prenatal care along with anticoagulant shots right from the start?"

"Yes," Sarah admitted. "But I feel so terrible about abandoning you."

"Please," she scoffed. "I'm a big girl. I have my itinerary and my French phrasebook."

Sarah winced. Lily had a terrible accent, being unable to master the sheer nasality of the language. "Well, at this time of year there are always English speakers roaming around if you get into a bind. And Curt and I will take you to the airport like we planned. I wish I had given you more notice than this," she fretted.

"I wouldn't change anything," Lily told her, and that was the truth. Later on in the pregnancy, when her cousin felt more secure, Lily would inform her she was going to be the godmother. Maybe she would bring back a little French toy for the baby and keep it hidden until he or she was born.

Curt loaded her things into the trunk and they headed for the Verrazano Bridge to cross into New York. JFK Airport sat on a bay overlooking the Atlantic Ocean in Queens. At that early hour, the miles passed quickly and Lily found herself deposited on the sidewalk with all her luggage.

Sarah reached her hand out the window to grab her cousin's hand. "Lily, Lily, please take care of yourself." Her eyes were filling up. Lily's were, too, only she didn't have early pregnancy hormones to blame, thank God.

She blew Sarah a kiss. "Everything will be fine. I'll text you once I land. You just concentrate on taking care of yourself—and your baby."

Sarah waved as Curt pulled away from the curb. Lily took a deep breath and hefted her backpack onto her shoulders before pulling her medium-size rolling suitcase into the terminal.

Her first major trip anywhere. France, land of wine and roses, perfume and pomp. Wow, that sounded good. She grabbed her phone and quickly entered that phrase. She had her laptop all tuned up and ready for the great stories that would fall in her lap.

Lily was going to take France by storm.

JACQUES MONTFORD HOPPED off the Métro stop a few blocks from the family mansion on Rue de Faubourg St-Honoré. His mother, the Dowager Countess de Brissard, had wanted to send the family car to meet him at the airport, but he needed more time. Time to get out of the closeness of the airplane, the craziness of Charles de Gaulle Airport, time to get some fresh air—as fresh as Paris could provide.

He climbed the stairs to the street. Ah, the *parfum de Paris* in the summer. More than a hint of auto exhaust and pollution, but also a touch of garden from behind the high walls he passed. Jasmine, definitely rose and a touch of lily. But no lavender.

The only lavender in Paris was in the buckets in the flower market and maybe in a clay pot in some less sophisticated neighborhood than the one he walked through.

For real lavender, Jacques would have to leave Paris and go to Provence.

The idea of another trip at that point seemed exhausting. More exhausting than staying with his mother in Paris? That remained to be seen.

He rounded the corner to the house and took the steps before knocking on the wide wooden door. He hadn't bothered to take his key ring on his trip to the Southeast Asian typhoon disaster area. As a relief-work physician, he'd had plenty of important medical supplies to carry with him. It was typical to bring one backpack of personal items and a couple of large suitcases filled with medicine, bandages and emergency surgical instruments. In fact, he was wearing his trusty backpack right now. He couldn't wait to drop it in his suite of rooms, take a shower and grab something to eat in the large kitchen. A quick knock, the door opened and he was officially in hell.

"Surprise!" A crowd full of people he didn't know greeted him, slapping him on the back and shaking his hand.

His mother, her hair an exact color match for his thanks to the hairdresser, fought her way to him, kissing him on both cheeks twice and crying prettily, though not enough to either ruin her mascara or redden her eyes. "Jacques! *Mon petit* Jacques is finally home!" she announced. His mother's guests cheered again.

He was a rich lady's prize poodle being trotted out for admiration. *And for his next trick, he will administer oral rehydration salts and give measles vaccinations!*

He felt like turning around and leaving. But the crowd filled in behind him and Bellamy was taking his beat-up backpack from him.

His mother clutched his shoulders. "Ah, Jacques, your hair. Why so long?" She fingered his long ponytail of chestnut-brown hair. "And *la barbe* that hides your handsome face?" She tapped his beard. "You look like one of those scruffy men who live in the subway." She, of course, was impeccably turned out in a flowing silk peach-colored lounge suit, the perfect outfit for an evening party at home.

"*Maman,* please." He took her hand away from his face but kissed the back of it so she wouldn't fuss.

She dimpled at him. "Someone else is waiting to kiss you," she said coyly.

He had no idea who. "Bellamy?" He was their ancient butler and the idea of being kissed by the old English fossil made him crack the first smile of the evening.

Unfortunately his mother misunderstood. "Oh, you funny boy. But that smile tells me you know who I mean."

"Actually, *Maman,* I don't…" he began, and then his teeth clicked together in shock at the person she intended him to kiss.

He'd rather have dysentery again.

"Nadine." It was difficult to pronounce his ex-fiancée's name from a clenched jaw, but he did just fine.

She took that as an invitation instead of an expression of dismay. "Oh, *mon amour!*" She flung her expensively dressed arms around his neck and tried to kiss him, but he turned his head and was happy to see her spitting out strands of his hair instead.

He took her by the upper arms and tried to set her away from him, but her grip reminded him of a gecko he'd watched while lying in a hospital bed in Thailand. That sticky-footed lizard could walk upside down on the ceiling and even across glass without falling. Of course it could also lick its eyes with its tongue, something that Nadine had not mastered—as far as he knew. What she did with her tongue was none of his business anymore. It was what she had done with it while it *had* been his business that had caused their breakup.

So why was she here, reenacting *The Hero's Welcome* from a black-and-white postwar movie? Jacques looked around at his proud mother and her well-lubricated guests eyeing him and beautiful blonde Nadine fondly. Nadine wisely decided not to kiss him again and instead threaded her arm through his, snuggling into his side. A hired waiter pressed a glass of champagne into his hand that wasn't suctioned to Nadine, and his mother raised her own glass.

"To my son, Jacques Charles Olivier Fortanier Montford, Comte de Brissard." As usual, she forgot the title he valued the most—doctor.

But the guests cheered anyway. Perhaps his beard hid what had to be a sour expression. *Huzzah, huzzah.* All that was needed was a rousing orchestral version of "La Marseillaise" as the weary warrior came limping back to Paris. He started to sing under his breath. *"Allons, enfants de la Patrie..."*

Nadine gave him a strange look and he remembered his precarious situation. She wanted nothing better than to be Madame la Comtesse de Brissard, and Jacques's paltry wishes were the only impediment to her desire to enter the *noblesse.*

He detached himself from Nadine and raised his glass in fake cheer when he caught his mother staring at them. "Come with me, Nadine."

He hurried her into the small hallway leading to the back stairs. Nadine looked at him apprehensively but reached out her arms to him.

Jacques folded his. "Nadine, what the hell are you doing here?" She started to pout, but he ignored it. "Were you hoping I'd developed amnesia along with dysentery?"

"Jacques!"

He was too tired to be kind anymore. "Go away, Nadine. I don't know what you've been telling my mother all these months, but it doesn't seem to have been the truth."

"But, *mon cher,* we just had a little misunderstanding before you left. If you had stayed instead of going to that dreadful typhoon, we would have smoothed things over in no time."

His jaw fell. "Nadine, I caught you having sex with your personal trainer. In our bed."

"I know, I know." She pasted an anguished expression

on her face. "And I feel terrible about that. I made a mistake."

I, I, I. Or as his Portuguese friend Francisco would say, *Ay, ay, ay.* It was all still about her.

"No, Nadine. We were through as soon as you undressed for that hairless, muscle-bound refugee from the tanning salon."

Her lips tightened, and he realized the Neckless Wonder might still be her "workout partner." She scoffed, apparently deciding to take the offensive. "Jacques, you know marriages among our class are not necessarily exclusive. Don't be so bourgeois."

"Genetically impossible, *chérie.* As you well know, I am the Count de Brissard," he taunted her.

The look in her eye made him glad the guillotine had been retired two hundred years ago. "You have the soul of a *peasant.*" And she meant it to sting.

Too bad for her he spoiled it by laughing. "I take that as a grand compliment. As a rule, peasants do not cheat and then have the gall to mock the person they cheat on." Although he had had a few months to come to terms with her infidelity, it still angered him and he started to raise his voice.

"You are the most selfish man I ever met!" she shouted at him.

"Selfish? Because I do not care to share my fiancée sexually?"

"Pah! If you would have stayed in France for more than two weeks, perhaps I wouldn't have needed to find companionship elsewhere."

"*Bien,* so I am selfish for leaving this mansion and going to the absolute hellholes of the world to help people who have nothing? Sick people? Dying people? *Et toi,* how do *you* help anyone but yourself?"

"Eh, *oui,* Saint Jacques of Paris. Any more of your 'good works' and they will be carving a statue of you for the Cathedral de Notre Dame. Make sure they get your sweaty hippie hair and beard correct. *Cochon!*" Her face reddened.

He didn't know if she was calling him a pig because of his hair or his personality, and he didn't care. "You are unbelievable. I am grateful I saw your true character before marrying you. I'm sure you would have cost me plenty to divorce you once I found out."

Her mouth twisted, about to fire more insults at him, but he couldn't take it—couldn't take *her*—any longer. He rounded the corner leading back to the party and stopped short.

His mother stood stricken in the hall, her hand covering her mouth—like he wished he had done to himself. The guests stood behind her, their expressions ranging from shocked to sly to amused.

Even Bellamy was shaking his dignified gray head. If Bellamy heard them yelling, they must have been loud indeed.

"Maman." He lowered his head to hers. "I am so sorry to ruin…" Out of the corner of his eye he caught a young man with disheveled blond hair surreptitiously taking his photo with his phone.

Was nothing private anymore? He couldn't even talk to his mother in their own home without some idiot and his camera phone?

"Eh, you!" he shouted at the man. "No photos. Give me that phone."

The guy clutched his phone to his chest but Jacques easily wrestled it from him and deleted the picture.

But that first man was not the only one. A larger camera took his picture—several times. Had his mother hired a photographer for the party? No, he noticed a polished brunette standing next to the photographer, taking copious notes.

"Reporters, *Maman?*"

Her stricken expression confirmed it. "Just the society page. They asked to come when we got news of your return."

"I don't want to be on the society page." That was a big reason he didn't stay in France for very long.

"I'm so sorry, Jacques." Her big blue eyes started to tear. "I missed you so much and wanted to welcome you back."

The large room started pressing in on him. "No, *Maman*, I'm sorry for embarrassing you. But I can't stay."

"What?" Her forehead creased. "But, Jacques, you just got home."

"I can't," he repeated. The noise, the bright lights, even the smell of the food was making him dizzy and disoriented. Nadine's theatrical sobs in the background didn't help, either. He pushed his way through the party guests and grabbed his beat-up backpack from near the door.

Ever the professional, Bellamy opened the door. "Good to see you again, milord," the butler informed him. Jacques gave him an incredulous glance considering the *mêlée* coming towards them, but the old man was as unruffled as always.

"If you would permit some advice from a longtime family retainer, I would recommend a sojourn in the country. Perhaps some fresh air and hearty cooking would benefit your constitution."

"That's the best idea I've heard in a long time, Bellamy. *Merci beaucoup.*" Jacques spotted the ambitious reporter and her photographer gaining on him.

"Not to fear, sir, mum's the word." After delivering the

quintessential English promise, Bellamy tipped him a wink before practically shoving him out the double doors.

Jacques darted down the steps and heard a thud against the door. Bellamy was holding off the savages at the pass, so to speak, so Jacques took advantage of the delay and made a beeline for the Métro.

He hopped a train to the Latin Quarter, a quirky neighborhood along the Seine that was home to the famous Sorbonne, the seat of the University of Paris. He knew of a student hostel there, and his scruffy appearance would blend right in. A bowl of soup in the café, a good night's sleep and then out of the city.

He'd had enough of Paris, and he'd only been there about two hours. A new record, even for him.

2

LILY STEPPED INTO the elevator of the youth hostel. At twenty-six, she was a bit older than many of the backpackers, but they were an accepting bunch. She'd never had the money to take a year off and backpack through Europe, so she envied the young students.

Two of them called down the bare-bones hallway to hold the elevator, so Lily stuck her arm out to block the doors.

"Thank you, Lily. Where do you go today?" Blonde and German, Silke and her companion, Hans, had been very helpful since Lily's arrival, pointing out tricks to getting around the Métro and giving her tips on cheap eats. To save money, Lily ate like the backpackers—rolls and *café au lait* at the bakery across the street for breakfast, a loaf of bread and ham along with some cheese and fresh fruit for lunch, and maybe a dinner out at a café if she could find one reasonably priced.

"I'm not exactly sure, but probably to *la Madeleine.*"

"Who?"

"*La Madeleine* is a giant church in the Opera Quarter. Napoleon helped design part of it." Lily's stomach growled. "Plus there's a huge food mall and flower market next to it."

"Ah, very good." She gestured to her equally blond companion. "Hans and I are going to the cemetery in Montparnasse."

Hans nodded enthusiastically. "*Ja,* many important writers and thinkers are buried there. Jean-Paul Sartre and Simone de Beauvoir, Charles Baudelaire and—"

"And don't forget Samuel Beckett. He wrote *Waiting For Godot,*" Silke added helpfully, in case Lily wasn't familiar with that mind-numbing play. Thanks to her English degree, she unfortunately was.

"And if we have enough time, we will see the Catacombes. When they ran out of room in the city cemetery a couple centuries ago, they moved everyone there."

"Everyone?" Surely they didn't mean…

"They have walls of skulls and bones. That says so much about what life is all about. In the end, we are just piles of organic matter for others to stare at," Silke finished.

Lily fought back a sigh. How very grimly existential of them. No wonder they were going into raptures about Sartre and Simone de Beauvoir, the king and queen of existentialism. Lily preferred to take a more cheerful view of life, but that didn't seem to be the European way. No wonder they thought Americans were cockeyed optimists. And of course most Americans, if they thought of the French at all, imagined either mimes in white-striped shirts or else morose chain-smoking café dwellers dressed all in black.

Maybe that was a good blog article. "So what do you think of Parisians?"

Silke immediately answered, "Oh, it is very nice here."

"*Ja,*" Hans agreed.

The elevator opened and they walked out to the lobby. "But what do you really think?" she insisted.

Silke looked around furtively. "It is not very organized. Sometimes the attractions do not open on time."

"Twenty minutes late, even," Hans threw in. "And they close for lunch at all hours—not what the sign says."

Lily smiled. Ah, punctuality. The more laidback French attitude did not sit right with German precision. "I can see how that would be a problem. But perhaps some spontaneity is a good thing on vacation?"

They gave her identically puzzled looks. Silke shrugged. "If they want to be open different hours, they should change the signs."

And that was that. Lily waved goodbye as they set off for their sunny Parisian day of skulls and cemeteries.

Lily turned toward the door, but she bumped into another backpacker, a tall, lean man with a long brown ponytail and matching beard. "Oh, *pardonnez-moi,*" she tried her French on him.

"No problem," he replied in perfect English with only a hint of an accent, as he adjusted the straps of his small black backpack.

Rats. "Is my accent that awful?" she burst out.

"What?" He looked at her, startled.

"My accent. My cousin Sarah says I have a terrible French accent, even on basic things like *pardonnez-moi* and *merci.*"

He gave a tiny wince as she pronounced those words.

"You hear it, too, don't you?" she cried. "I must sound like the American village idiot trying to speak your language."

"Hey, hey," he soothed her. "How long have you been living in France?"

"I've been visiting for a couple days."

He raised his shoulders in a typically French shrug.

"And so you think your two days in Paris means you speak French perfectly?"

"Well, I guess not. But you speak English perfectly."

"I should hope so. I lived in Manhattan for ten years."

"Really? I'm from Philly, but I live in New Jersey right now."

"Ah, Joisey," he said in a perfect New Jersey accent. Was there no accent this man couldn't do?

"Hey, don't knock Jersey. Not all of us can afford Manhattan." Although he didn't look like he could afford even the student hostel. And if he'd lived in New York for ten years, he was probably older than the other backpackers, too.

He held up his hands in placation. They were big and nicely shaped, with long, strong-looking fingers.

"Do you play piano?"

"What?" He looked startled again. Lily was single-handedly earning a reputation for all Americans as being slightly crazy.

"Piano." She wiggled her fingers at him.

He looked down at his hands and then back at her. "Why? Do you want me to play a tune for you? Would you like 'Alouette' or 'Frère Jacques'?"

"I can see you must be too busy to make conversation." She lifted her nose like she'd seen her mother's employer do a million times before to an impudent guest. Mrs. Wyndham was one of the grand ladies of Philadelphia's upper crust and Lily's mother was still her housekeeper, in charge of managing the myriad employees and tasks necessary for the smooth running of a historic mansion and busy social activities. "Thank you for your assistance, and have a nice day."

She brushed past him out the door onto the busy French sidewalk. Fresh croissant or *pain au chocolat* for breakfast?

Flaky French chocolate rolls sounded good. Before she could decide, she felt a touch on her elbow.

"Hey, hey." Backpack Guy stopped touching her with his long piano fingers as soon as she stood still. "I'm sorry, *mademoiselle.* You caught me by surprise and I forgot my manners."

"No problem." Lily spotted a café down the street that she hadn't visited yet. "I'm always grumpy before breakfast, and that chocolate roll is calling my name." She eyed his spare frame. She didn't think it was from too many cigarettes since he didn't smell of smoke. In fact, for a guy who looked like he'd been sleeping on a park bench for a month, he actually smelled nice. "If you don't mind my saying so, you could use a croissant."

His mouth pulled into a wry grin. "Probably. Why don't we get some croissants together?"

She leaned away from him and gave him a suspicious stare.

"I was a Boy Scout if that makes a difference."

"Really? There are French Boy Scouts?" She perked up. This was the kind of thing she wanted to learn about his country—something that wasn't in the tourist books.

"Come have a *café au lait* with me and I'll tell you all about *le scoutisme français.*"

"*Scoutisme?* Is that a real word?"

"On my honor." He raised his hand in what looked like a Boy Scout sign.

"Well, okay. And maybe you can help me with my French pronunciation."

"I would be happy to."

Lily turned to face him. "All right, I can't call you French Backpacking Boy Scout, so you better tell me your name."

He smothered a laugh. "No, that would be quite a mouthful. My name is Jack Montford."

"Jack? Isn't it actually Jacques?"

"Yes, but I started going by Jack when I lived in New York."

"Smart move. I'm Lily Adams." Lily set off for the café. "Come on, Jack-with-the-Backpack, let's get you a couple croissants—with extra butter."

JACK DIDN'T KNOW quite how he'd wound up going out for breakfast with a woman he'd literally bumped into, but Lily Adams was right—he could use some calories. She'd thought he picked her out as an American from her accent, bad as it was, but he had picked her out as an American as soon as he saw her blond ponytail and cheerful expression. Her hazel-green eyes gazed eagerly at everything, as if she were trying to memorize details for later.

And to think she wanted to learn about French scouting, of all things. Not where to get the best-smelling *parfum* or cheapest designer knockoffs, but actual bits of real French life.

They stepped up to the café counter and Lily cleared her throat. *"Je voudrais deux croissants et deux pains au chocolat. Oh, deux cafés au lait. Merci."*

Jack had to admire her tenacity when she knew she had difficulties with the language. He quelled the cashier's incipient smirk with what he thought of his *comte* look.

Lily, happily oblivious, accepted the bag of pastries and handed him a cup of coffee.

"Merci," he thanked her. "And you say *de rien,* which means, 'It was nothing.'"

She practiced that a couple times as they walked to a bench along a pretty little park. Jack chewed a bit of *pain au chocolat,* mindful that his digestion was still a bit sensitive. Lily dipped her croissant into the milky coffee with gusto, not minding the flaky crumbs falling on her khaki cargo pants.

University students from the nearby Sorbonne argued about philosophy and politics while a young long-haired musician played guitar, his girlfriend staring up at him adoringly.

Nadine had stared at him like that while they were dating, but stopped soon after their engagement. It was as if she didn't need to bother once she had his ring. And of course he had been gone many months out of the year with his disaster relief work. His closest friends in the world, Giorgio, Prince of Vinciguerra, and Francisco, Duke of Aguas Santas in Portugal, had warned him to slow down.

Jack found it easy to ignore their advice. They were ones to talk about slowing down. Giorgio ran his own country and Francisco owned not only a huge, busy estate in the Portuguese countryside but also a private island in the Azores.

If only his friends had grabbed him in person a couple months back, since it wasn't hard to delete their phone and text messages.

He'd slowed down, all right, almost to the point of permanently stopping. When they'd heard he was sick, George and Frank first offered to fly to the hospital in Thailand to collect him. When that hadn't been necessary, they threatened to confiscate his passport so he couldn't leave France until George's sister's wedding.

George, Frank and Jack had met going to university in New York and had set up a nice bachelor pad for themselves when George's parents tragically died in a car crash back in their small country Vinciguerra, on the Italian peninsula. George's distraught twelve-year-old sister, Stefania, had come to live with them, along with a no-nonsense housekeeper.

End of their bachelor pad, but the beginning of the best time of his life. Stevie became one of the gang and the sister he'd never had. And now she was getting married.

Jack hoped she and her German fiancé looked at each other like the young guitar player and his girlfriend.

"Earth to Jack." Lily peered into his face and waved a croissant. "You still hungry? You put away that chocolate roll pretty fast."

He looked down into his lap. A small pile of crumbs was all that remained. Maybe the fresh air and quiet greenery was helping his appetite, but he didn't want to push his luck. "You want to know about the real France?"

She rolled her eyes. "Of course. Who doesn't?"

"Many people. For them, we are France-Land, a giant amusement theme park for them to visit. See the Eiffel, look at the Mona Lisa, hear the bells rung by the Hunchback of Notre Dame, and *voilà!* You have experienced the true France."

She gave him a peeved look. "I don't agree with that at all, and you have a pretty low opinion of tourists for a guy who's backpacking his way around the country. Or is it just a low opinion of American tourists?"

"Well…"

"Aha. You, *monsieur,* are a snob. And see, I know that is a French word, too."

"I am not a snob." He was acquainted with many snobs and he wasn't one, was he?

"When you lived in New York, did you go to the Statue of Liberty?"

"Of course. A gift from my country to yours." Stevie had loved the green lady. If she hadn't been Princess of

Vinciguerra, Jack often thought, she would have become an American citizen.

"And the Metropolitan Museum of Art? And the Empire State Building?"

"Yes to all of those."

"So why can't we enjoy the Eiffel Tower, the Mona Lisa and the bells at Notre Dame Cathedral?"

He gave her a nod of apology. "Again, you have caught me without my manners. We are notably proud of those three things in Paris, and many more, of course."

"So since I have already visited all those places, tell me where I should go next to get a sense of the real France."

Jack made a split-second decision. His other belongings were safely stashed in a locker at the hostel for the day and he hadn't made any firm plans to leave for Provence. What was one more day? The trains were always running to the south of France. "Why don't I show you?"

Her pretty brow wrinkled again. "Show me what?"

"One of the most beautiful parks in Paris that only the locals know about. You like to hike?"

"I love it," she promptly replied. "The Appalachian Trail runs through Pennsylvania, and I've hiked several parts of it."

"Good, this will be easy for you. Do you have a Métro card?"

"All set." She stood and dumped her empty cup into a nearby trash can. "*Allons!* Let's go."

Jack smiled. Her dreadful accent was starting to seem rather cute. He immediately put the brakes on that idea. Lily was a tourist, and he was going back to Provence to sit in the sun, eat and regain his strength.

He grimaced. Kind of like the mangy stray cat his Provençal housekeeper Marthe-Louise had taken in and fattened up last winter. Ah, well, she'd be happy to do the same for him.

3

"I can't believe this is in the middle of the city." Lily gazed around the park in rapture. Fashionable young mothers in silk T-shirts and slim Capri cargo pants pushed babies in strollers, their gladiator sandals slapping the pavement. Older men strolled along the paths, conversing with enough upper body movement to qualify for a cardiovascular work-out. She was the only tourist in sight. "How do you say the name again? The sign says Butts, but that can't be right."

"No, we have no 'butts' here."

Lily sneaked a look at his, but those baggy shorts made it impossible to tell. Probably as lean as the rest of him. Rats! He caught her peeking. She fought a blush, and she hadn't even seen anything. He was kind of cute with his warm brown eyes.

"You would pronounce it 'Boot show-mon.'"

Lily never would have guessed that from the sign that read Parc des Buttes-Chaumont. "What does it mean?"

"*Buttes* are hills and *Chaumont* probably means 'bald mountain.' And *parc* means—"

She elbowed him, interrupting his chuckle. "Yes, thank you, I figured that out for myself."

He wrapped his arm around her shoulders for a brief

squeeze and then dropped it. "I am just teasing you, Lily. I admire your courage in coming by yourself to a country where you do not speak the language."

"I wouldn't have been on my own if my cousin hadn't had wonderful news." She found herself telling him about Sarah's past problems having a baby, and he nodded as if he knew what she was talking about.

"Yes, yes, it was wise for her to stay at home. Pregnancy can be difficult in the first trimester, especially with a history of complications." He cleared his throat. "But of course I am not an obstetrician."

She laughed. He looked as little like any ob-gyn she'd ever met. She pulled out her camera and took a few shots of Parisians enjoying the fine summer day. "Come on, let's walk." She followed the path into the park and was surprised to find herself in almost a forest. "Wow, Jack, look at all these trees."

"Yes, the park was commissioned by Napoleon III in the mid-1800s. Many of the trees were planted then." Jack pointed to a curve. "Ah, turn here."

All the noise of Paris had fallen away as they passed a red brick mansion in the park and crossed a terra-cotta-tiled bridge. "Down the steps?" Lily peered down a dark, cool tunnel.

"Exactement." Jack went down a couple steep steps and extended his hand. "Watch your step. The rock can be slippery."

Lily took his strong, warm hand. As they descended, she was grateful for his steady grip and her sturdy hiking boots. "How on earth did they ever make this park?"

"They shaped it from an old quarry and it took several years to finish."

She concentrated on keeping her footing and only looked up when they emerged onto a long, narrow suspension bridge. It was as if they were in a misty watercolor illustration of a fantasy novel heavy with wizards and princesses. She couldn't resist taking more photos, this time one-handed.

The bridge towered over a serene lake that reflected up the greens, yellows and reds of the surrounding trees. She realized they were still holding hands, but didn't let go. She'd enjoyed Paris, but missed Sarah badly. Sightseeing by herself wasn't as much fun as with someone else. A travel buddy gave her the chance to say, *Wow, look at that,* or even spotting something funny and giving a nudge to share in the joke.

Lily looked sideways at Jack and was surprised to see how much he had relaxed. "You're not much of a city boy, are you?" They started to cross the wooden planks of the bridge, the steel railings making decorative geometric patterns of triangles and rectangles.

He smiled, his white teeth showing through his thick beard. She wondered what he looked like under all that hair. Just her luck, he would have no chin or a weird facial tattoo. "No, I would rather be in the country. Once I have finished in Paris, I am going south, to Provence."

"Provence," she tested the name on her tongue. "You're from there."

"My family is. I don't get there as often as I like." He cleared his throat. "But enough about me. What do you do when you are not traveling?"

Hmm. She didn't want to tell him she was writing travel articles because he might worry she was writing down everything he said. "I'm a freelance writer. I write magazine and newspaper articles on anything I can get paid for—history, local sights—I've even covered school-board meetings and supermarket grand openings."

"Ah." He nodded thoughtfully.

"What, *ah?*"

"That is why you want to learn about the real Paris, the real France. People interest you as much as the places."

"Hmm. I've never thought of it that way. I just wanted to keep busy and keep getting jobs." They came to the end of the bridge and Lily pulled her hand free from his, pointing up to the Roman temple-looking thing on the hill in front of them. "Wow, look at that." She supposed she could have used her other hand to point, but she was starting to like holding his hand a little too much.

Her danger signals were flashing: romantic park setting in Paris—*check.* Hand-holding with a well-spoken, seemingly decent guy—*check.* Not remembering the last time she held any male body part—*check.*

Jack pulled a water bottle from his small backpack and drank. "One more thing to see before we climb." He took a deep breath and headed down the trail toward the lake.

Lily fought a pang of irrational disappointment that he didn't take her hand again, but the man obviously could read mixed signals as fast as she sent them. She followed Jack and stopped next to a weeping willow tree, its yellowish branches and silvery green leaves drooping over the path. "Sing willow, willow, willow. Sing all a green willow will be my garland." She couldn't help grabbing a handful of branches and clutching them to her in pure dramatic fashion. She was such an English major geek.

Jack stopped. "*Othello,* right?"

Her jaw fell. He wasn't even a native English speaker and he knew enough Shakespeare to understand her obscure reference? "Very good." She sounded like Sarah at her most teacher-ish.

"Shakespeare in the Park." Central Park, NYC, that is. He started walking again.

"I went to that once! But they did one of the comedies, not a tragedy. Which do you like better?"

"The comedies, of course. Real life has enough sadness already."

"True. And I never liked the character of Othello. He had everything he ever wanted and tossed it away because Iago preyed on his insecurities. Weak." She shook her head. "And strangling his wife, Desdemona—what a creep."

"The man did die by his own hand in the end," Jack pointed out.

"He should have done everyone a favor and done that first. Or *maybe* he could have even believed his wife was telling the truth about being faithful to him and then gone and kicked Iago's ass for making trouble."

"Unfortunately, marital fidelity and ass-kicking make for dull theater."

"Not if they have a good fight choreographer for the ass-kicking scene. Those guys can make thumb-wrestling look fascinating."

"Thumb-wrestling?"

Aha, so there was at least one American tradition he didn't know about. She was about to lift her hand to show him but realized they'd be holding hands again, albeit in a combative manner. "I'll show you later." She dropped the willow branches and turned toward the sound of rushing water.

Jack stood there gazing up at the tree. "Aspirin is derived from willow bark—the scientific name salicylic acid comes from the willow genus *Salix*."

She turned slowly to stare at him. "How do you know that?"

"Science class."

Lily raised her eyebrows. "You must have paid better

attention in science class than I did." She was lucky to recall that the scientific name for humans was *Homo sapiens.*

"I know you have your own strengths." He moved close and for a second, she thought he would kiss her under the umbrella of the bowing branches. But he must have picked up her hesitation again and withdrew, the gleam in his brown eyes shuttered. "*Allons!* Let's go see the waterfall."

"Okay." She followed him, expecting to see a stream burbling over a shallow drop, but instead they stepped into another grotto, with a high waterfall thundering down to a pool at their feet. "Holy cow, look at that. And this is part of that same quarry?"

He nodded and tipped his face up to the water, little droplets condensing on his cheeks. She closed her eyes and did the same, exhaling deeply as some of her tension flowed away.

Traveling without Sarah had been more stressful than she realized. She had to be constantly alert to where she was and who she was near. And the language barrier—well, that wasn't so bad. Sarah had been right that there were plenty of English speakers roaming Paris.

Like Jack. He was a bit of a puzzle—scruffy-looking but clean and obviously well-educated with a variety of knowledge. She opened her eyes to find him watching her with an enigmatic expression.

"You rarely find places like this in any city."

"No." She shook her head in agreement. "There's nothing like it in Philadelphia or New York."

"That is a replica of the Roman temple of Daphne." He pointed up to the round Grecian-looking building. "It's the highest point in the park and you can see all the way across Paris to the Sacre-Coeur Cathedral."

"Great!" Lily checked her camera to make sure she had

plenty of space on her memory card and set off after him. The stairs were cut into the rock as before and twisted around as they ascended. She was so excited that she didn't realize Jack had fallen behind. He waved her on when she stopped. "Just getting a drink—I'll catch up to you in a minute."

She was too excited to drink and quickly got to the top. "Oh," she gasped. It was just as Jack had said, the best view in the city. She looked down on all the cute neighborhoods and across northeast Paris to the white dome of Sacre-Coeur Cathedral. She grabbed her camera and took shots from every angle, zooming in on the cathedral and the houses below. The bridge made a cool composition with the surrounding trees reflecting in the water. "'A favorite of local Parisians, Parc Butts-Something-Or-Other is a hidden treasure of greenery amidst the noisy city.'" Yes, that introductory sentence sounded pretty good, so she typed it into her phone.

But where was Jack? She peered around guiltily at being so caught up in her work. Had he twisted his ankle? "Jack?" she called, descending several steps. He stood below her, huffing and puffing.

"Stopped to take a drink." He limped up the rest of the stairs.

"Hey, you're gasping. Are you okay?"

"Fine," he gritted out, bending over to rest his hands on his knees and sucking air at a pretty good pace.

Lily looked around, wondering what she should do if he keeled over. They were alone at the highest point of the park and she couldn't exactly toss him over her shoulder in a fireman's carry. "Do you need an inhaler?"

He shook his head. At least he wasn't asthmatic. She could see herself calling the Parisian version of 911 and trying to ask for emergency medical help to come to some park with the word *butts* in the name.

He straightened, his face flushed with exertion and probably embarrassment, too. He pulled a bottle of water from his small backpack and sipped slowly.

She pulled out her own water and pretended they had stopped for a water break. Once he wiped his mouth and met her glance, she shook her head. "Too many cigarettes will kill your endurance."

He gave a dry laugh that turned into a cough at the end. "I am not a smoker, Lily. I am probably the only man in France who doesn't smoke."

She had to agree with him there. The tobacco-free movement was about as welcome as a barge of plague rats floating down the Seine. "Well, you've got that going for you."

"But not much else, eh?" His color seemed to be returning to normal. He spread his arms wide. "Ah, the perfect specimen of French manhood. I cannot even climb a hill without gasping like an old man with emphysema."

"Have you been sick?"

Jack sighed. "Unfortunately, but I was hoping I was better."

"Maybe you're pushing it a bit to come to the hilliest point in Paris, don't you think?"

He grimaced. "You are right. I should have known better."

"What are you getting over, if you don't mind my asking?" She hoped it was nothing awful like cancer or something serious like that.

The first glimmer of humor returned to his brown eyes. "Dysentery."

"Dysentery?" she blurted. She found herself unconsciously stepping back from him, trying to remember if they had shared any food or drink. "How in the world do you get dysentery these days? I thought the tap water smelled a bit funny but I thought it was okay to drink." Was that why everyone carried bottles of expensive spring water? Why didn't Sarah mention this to her before she left? *Don't drink the water!* Wasn't that usually the last advice people shouted out the windows of their cars as they dropped you off at the airport for a journey to a foreign country?

"No, I did not get dysentery in France." He rubbed his cheek as if his beard itched. "I caught it in Myanmar."

"Myanmar? Why on earth would you go there?" She'd never heard anything good about that place nowadays, ever since they stopped calling it Burma. It was definitely not on her list of places to visit.

Jack set off at an easy walk and Lily followed him. "They had a typhoon and I was an aid worker—food, shelter, healthcare, all the fundamental necessities. I accidentally drank some untreated water and…" He held out his arms. *"Voilà."*

"Wow, you went there on purpose?" She realized that sounded kind of rude. "I mean, that's noble work."

"Not so noble when you get as sick as the people you are trying to help. I wasted many resources, especially when they had to take me to the hospital in Thailand."

"You must have been severely ill, then."

"Eh, there were many who would have benefited from hospital care but I was the one who was transferred out."

"Guilt." She raised her index finger to make her point. "You have survivor's guilt."

"What?" He gave her a funny look.

"Sure. You're thinking, 'Why me? Why did I get better medical treatment than the others? Why did I live when others didn't?'"

He glanced down and away from her. "You may be right."

"And what are the answers to those questions?" Lily gave an imitation-French shrug. "No one knows. Come on, you're French. Use a little bit of that national tendency toward fatalism. It was meant to happen that way." She peered into his face and gasped in pretend shock. "Surely you're not an *optimist,* are you?"

A small smile crept across his lips. "Well…"

"Uh-oh." She wagged her finger. "Watch out—someone might mistake you for an American if you're not careful. An optimistic Frenchman. Tsk, tsk, who would have thought?"

"A personal failing." He grinned at her. "Please do not tell anyone. I would like to keep my French passport."

"Don't let it happen again. If French people were all cheerful and friendly, what would tourists complain about?"

"Parisians are Parisians." He gave that uniquely French shrug that she had tried to copy and failed. "You will find if you go to different areas of the country, people are more friendly."

"Like Provence?"

His face softened and he wore a faraway glance. "Exactly. The air is warm and light and the sky is pure blue. The hills are always green, and even the north wind, the *mistral,* brings clear, dry weather in its path."

Lily was memorizing his description as best as she could, his words painting a vivid picture.

"Everything is more in Provence. The food is richer, the wine is crisper, the fish are bigger and the ducks are plumper. Have you ever had a day where everything comes together—the weather, the countryside and the food?"

Lily did. "Once, my mother and I packed a picnic and

drove out to Washington Crossing Historic Park, where George Washington crossed the Delaware River to capture Trenton from the English. There is a huge wildflower preserve on the grounds, and Mom and I sat in the middle of the flowers, smelling the perfume, listening to the bees. The sky was bright blue with white puffy clouds and we ate chocolate éclairs and licked the melted smears off our fingers." Funny how she hadn't remembered that outing in so long. Despite her mother's busy schedule, she carved out time to spend with Lily.

"Almost every day is like that in the Provençal countryside." He sighed. "I have been away too long. But soon I will return."

JACK FELT SLIGHTLY better talking about Provence, but the rest of his morning had been a severe humiliation. He'd finally caught his breath descending from the beautiful Grecian folly, but not without several worried looks from the lovely Lily, who fussed over him as if he were an old man.

He was a man who could land a twin-engine plane on a grass airstrip and immediately trek several miles through harsh jungle terrain, but he couldn't manage a set of stairs in the middle of Paris. *Pathétique.*

But look, there was someone in worse shape than him. He stopped next to a young mother trying to carry her baby down the last set of stairs in one arm and her bulky carriage hooked over her other elbow. "May I help?"

The woman nodded gratefully and handed over the carriage. He carried it down for her but realized he was breathing hard and sweating again. How embarrassing, especially when Lily noticed, as well.

"Careful, Jack, you're still getting over that case of dysentery."

Unfortunately, *dysentery* in English translated to

dysenterie in French and the young mother gave him a look of horror, yanking her carriage away.

"No, no, *madame*. I am all better now," he tried to soothe her in French. She still looked panicked. "Trust me, I am a physician myself."

"Then you should know better, *monsieur*. You should not be going about Paris infecting innocent mothers and babies." She glared at him and scurried away, baby still in one arm and pushing the carriage with a couple fingertips—probably home to disinfect everything he touched.

He sighed. "Lily, you can't go around telling people I have dysentery. It makes them nervous." That was an understatement. Instead of Typhoid Mary, he was Dysentery Jack.

"You mean she understood me?" she asked eagerly.

"The word is almost the same in both languages."

"Oh. Sorry."

"For that word, you have a perfect French accent."

"Figures." She laughed. "What are some other diseases I can learn in French and terrorize the local populace? How about dengue fever?"

He had to laugh in return. Oh, boy, did he know diseases. Most of them had been eradicated in developed countries, fortunately. "That would be *la dengue*."

"Ho-hum. Typhoid?"

"Typhoïde."

"Boring. Diphtheria?"

"Diphtérie."

"Bubonic plague?"

Ah, he'd barely escaped an outbreak in Madagascar that had popped up just after his team had left a flood scene. Thanks to some heavy-duty antibiotics given in case, none of them had gotten sick. "That is *la peste bubonique*."

"Really?" Her smooth forehead wrinkled. "You French

must be pretty cool customers. Plague is a mere pest for you. And I know more French than I thought. Since you don't want me telling people you're getting over dysentery, if anyone asks me what's bothering you, I can tell them you have *la dengue, typhoïde, dipthérie* or even *la peste bubonique*."

He groaned, imagining the frantic calls to the Ministry of Health and the tabloid articles—*The Count of Brissard, recently returned from a mysterious hospitalization in Thailand, is rumored to be carrying dengue fever, typhoid, diphtheria and bubonic plague.* "Please do not. I have no desire to be thrown in quarantine for undetermined weeks. I spent enough time in the hospital already."

"Okay, okay, I'm only kidding. You're the only person I know in this whole country. I certainly don't want you quarantined."

"Good. Although I will have to keep on your good side, just in case."

Lily laughed, the sound light and carefree. He hadn't heard nearly enough laughter in how long? Months? There hadn't been much to laugh about in typhoon country.

He wanted to hear more of Lily's laughter. Before his rational, scientific mind could censor his previously undiscovered impulsive side, he blurted, "Come to Provence with me. You want to see the real France? I will show it to you."

4

Lily swirled her pale golden chardonnay as she sat in a café across from the hostel. Its motion was almost hypnotic as it circled the glass. She was being more pensive than usual, but really, what was the point if you couldn't visit Paris and wax philosophic over a glass of wine?

And she had plenty to think about. Coming to Paris alone had strained the boundaries of her capacity for adventure, but to set off for Provence with a near-stranger? Her warning bells were sending off a few clangs, and unfortunately, being the imaginative type, she could imagine the headlines: American Writer Disappears in Provence; in Unrelated news, the Grape Harvest Is Unusually Heavy in One Lonely Vineyard. Or, Notorious French Criminal Claims to be Aid Worker Recovering from Dysentery. Or would that be *dysenterie?*

But Provence…ooh la la. Summer in the South of France. Perfume, lavender, roses. She was really starting to love France and had even bought some new clothes to better fit in. Tonight she was wearing a floaty peach-colored silk top and a khaki miniskirt—even a pair of the gladiator sandals that she'd seen everywhere.

"Is this seat taken?" a familiar male voice asked.

Lily looked up from her wine. Was that…no, it couldn't be, but it was. "Jack, what did you do with your hair?" she blurted.

"It's in the wastebasket of a barber who wore almost the same look of horror when he first saw me."

No, not horror. Shock and amazement that he would cover up such a nice face with a mop of hair. He was way past good-looking and into the handsome realm. She'd thought he was nice-looking in a kind of shaggy, granola-crunchy way before, but minus the surplus hair? He was downright sexy.

Of course he was a bit pale where his beard had covered, and still a bit too thin, but that actually made him look like he should be modeling fashionable skinny jeans and snug dress shirts with an expression of ineffable ennui.

"What is that?" She stared at his chin. "Do you have a dimple in your chin?"

He sat down across from her. "Hush. Men don't have dimpled chins, they have cleft chins." The waiter appeared and Jack ordered a chardonnay as well. "Would you like another? My treat."

"If you're sure you have money after your haircut." Everything in Paris was hideously overpriced, even barbers and basic chardonnay.

He smiled and her jaw dropped. She pointed a finger at him. "You have dimples in your cheeks, too—and don't tell me they're clefts. I majored in English and there's no such thing as a cleft cheek." He broke into laughter and her heart was pounding.

Oh, boy. His warm, golden-brown eyes lit up and his white, even teeth gleamed in the fading light.

"Ah, Lily, Lily." He used the French pronunciation of her name—Lee-lee. "I have laughed more with you today than I have in the past month."

"Laughter is the best medicine. Chardonnay is the second-best," she quipped as the waiter set down two more glasses.

He raised his glass in a toast. "*À votre santé.* To your health."

She touched her rim to his and drank. He did the same, stared at the wine and wagged his hand back and forth. "Eh, pretty good. You like white better than red?"

"Depends on what the meal is."

"But of course." He started to fiddle with his hair and dropped his hand sheepishly when it wasn't there. "Anyway, I realized that I probably startled you earlier when I invited you to Provence."

"A bit," Lily allowed, strangely disappointed that he might be rescinding his offer—an offer she wasn't seriously considering. Was she?

"Me, I am normally not so impulsive, but I thought if you wanted to see Provence, and I am going there, well, we could travel together. As friends, of course," he hastily added.

"Ah." She'd been attracted to his smart personality despite his shaggy looks—not her usual type at all. But clean-shaven and fashionably trimmed, he was a dangerous combo. "Look." She spread her hands. "You seem like a nice guy, but I didn't just fall off the turnip truck."

He leaned forward. "That is a fascinating American colloquialism. I've never heard that before. It means that you are not naive, no?"

"No. I mean, yes, I am not naive." His French-like use of double negatives was confusing her. "So why would I think it is a good idea to travel alone several hundred miles into remote countryside with a man I met this morning?"

"Of course!" He grinned. "You want my references. This is a very French custom."

"Always glad to be culturally accurate," she said dryly. "But really, you're going to call your friends François or Gérard so they can tell me what a good guy you are? Men will say anything to help other men."

"Pah." He made a disparaging gesture with his free hand. "Men like that are *cochons*. That is a very useful word to know. *Pigs.* Or *swine* if you are in a more poetic mood. But I have an impeccable reference who would vouch for my good character and lack of maniacal tendencies."

"I don't know about the maniacal tendencies. You did go to Myanmar during a typhoon."

"*After* a typhoon." He waggled his finger at her. "There is a grand difference."

"Well, you learned your lesson this time. At least in Provence you can drink the water."

"Why would you, with all the good wine?" He laughed. "Does your laptop have a webcam?"

"Sure." She'd "called" Sarah with it yesterday to assure her cousin she was still alive and walking around Paris. Sarah was still queasy, but that was the worst of it. Her OB had seen her the next day and had been horrified at the idea of an overseas trip.

"If I could borrow it, I can call one of my old teachers who would vouch for me. A lady teacher, if that would be better."

It would. Still not believing she was even considering a crazy side trip like this, Lily fired up the webcam and Jack dragged his chair around next to her. The tables were close together as it was, so he was only inches away.

Up close, he was even sexier as he rested his arm along the back of her chair. She inhaled his woodsy cologne that smelled exotic and…erotic. Her nipples tightened under her thin silk T-shirt, and a long-forgotten throbbing started between her thighs. She crossed her legs to try to tamp that down and forgot she was wearing a skirt and that he was sitting so close.

Her bare leg briefly rested on his thigh—he was still wearing shorts. She pulled away but instead wound up running her calf down the length of his.

That certainly did not help her cool off. Or him, either, apparently. His eyes widened and his nostrils flared. Geez, why didn't she just crawl into the guy's lap?

"Sorry," she muttered.

"No, no, it is very close in here." He took a deep breath and shifted away slightly before turning the computer toward him. "I have an account, so you will not be charged." He logged in and tapped in a web address. "Ah, here we are. Perhaps my former teacher is online now."

The wine in Lily's stomach hadn't sedated the butterflies as she waited for the window to open. What would she decide if she found out Jack Montford was the best thing since sliced croissants?

JACK'S FORMER GOVERNESS appeared in the webcam window on the computer screen. Her gray hair was pulled into a bun as usual, a pencil shoved into it. She was probably working on another editing or translating project from her home in London.

"*Bonsoir,* Madame Finch. How are you tonight?" he continued in French.

"Jacques, it is good to see you in one piece," she replied. "Why are we speaking in French?" Madame Finch was as English as Winston Churchill and had been Jack's governess for many years until he had gone to prep school. They almost never spoke French together because he had needed to practice his English.

"I need you to vouch for my good character to this young lady."

"What?" She wrinkled her brow. "You've never needed my help before to meet women. Surely your sterling personal qualities combined with the cachet of being the Count de Brissard are sufficient to impress the female sex?"

"Madame, I haven't told her about my title. She is suspicious of upper-class men as it is."

"Oh, a smart girl." Madame smirked.

Lily was starting to wonder why they were only speaking French. "So, Madame, I need to assure her of my sterling personal characteristics. Oh, and don't tell her I'm a doctor. She thinks I'm a regular disaster-relief worker."

"Anything else?" she asked dryly. "You must really want her to like you for yourself."

He stopped, struck by the truth of that statement. "Yes, yes, I do."

"If you like her so much, you must tell her about your whole life, more than bits and pieces."

"I will." Madame was correct, as always.

"Good." She switched into English. "Please do excuse our rudeness in speaking French in front of you, *mademoiselle.* I work as a French translator and editor and welcome any practice with a native speaker like Jacques."

Lily smiled. "No problem. I'm Lily Adams, from Philadelphia, but I live in New Jersey now."

Madame nodded. "Ah, an American. Jacques did enjoy his years there. I am Fiona Finch, and I was fortunate enough to be Jacques's teacher when he was young."

Good. She hadn't called herself the governess. That would have raised certain issues.

Lily cleared her throat. "Yes, well, Jack and I just met today."

Madame's eyebrows shot up. "Today? Well, a true *coup de foudre,* right, Jacques?"

"Oh, what does that mean?" Lily asked him innocently.

He gave a strained smile. "A flash of lightning, something unexpected." It also meant love at first sight.

"Yes, that's true." Lily smiled at Madame. "I bumped into him in the hostel lobby, tried practicing my French on him, and he responded in English because my French is obviously not very good. Then we started chatting, he took me to that park with *butts* in the name, and then he asked me to go to Provence with him. But I'm not going anywhere with a guy I met today because I don't want to be one of those international stories that wind up on the twenty-four-hour news networks discussing, 'Where could Lily Adams be?'" Lily wound down her worries, Madame nodding in agreement the whole time.

"I commend you for your sensibility. Unfortunately, Europe is full of handsome, unscrupulous young men."

Jack made a noise of protest, but Lily ignored him, leaning in to peer at Madame. "That's it exactly! I wasn't planning to come by myself but my cousin is having a baby, after all, and she wants me to be very careful because I am alone."

"You brave girl." Madame was ignoring him now as well in a moment of female bonding. "Cads and bounders! Europe's crawling with 'em these days. It's a wonder girls don't go missing by the trainloads considering the trash that dares walk the street."

"Exactly!"

Jack didn't see this going well for him. "But Madame—"

Madame was just warming up. "You should have seen the riffraff I encountered on my last trip. Utterly disgusting the way they act—"

"Madame, please!" Jack interrupted in desperation. "Lily is going to think I'm an axe murderer."

Both women looked at him as if they'd forgotten his presence. Lily muffled a giggle and Madame frowned at him for his poor manners.

"Excuse me, Madame," he apologized.

She sniffed but inclined her head in acceptance of his apology. "So, Mademoiselle Lily, despite the preponderance of dubious characters, my former student Jacques is not one of them. He is diligent, hard-working, courteous and of the highest moral fiber."

"He did say he was a Boy Scout."

"Oh, my, yes. Earned the highest award in the organization. If he has promised to show you around Provence, you can be assured that he will conduct himself with the utmost of gentlemanly qualities. No need to fear he would pounce on you like a panther."

"Oh." Was it his wishful thinking, or did Lily sound a tiny bit disappointed? She sat up straighter. "I'm glad you vouch for his character."

"Absolutely." Madame gave him a steely glare. "And I will give you my phone number. Please call me if you have any concerns. I have many friends in the south of France and they would be happy to come to your assistance." Jack winced—he'd better behave himself. Madame's friends in the south of France were all his own friends and employees, as well.

"That would be wonderful." Lily pulled out her cell phone and entered not only Madame's two phone numbers, but her email address and home address.

"There." His former governess sat back in satisfaction. "You're as safe as you would be with your cousin, my dear. Master Jacques will care for you as if you were his own sister."

"Of course." He gritted out a smile. He didn't have any sisters, and he certainly didn't consider Lily as one. But a promise was a promise.

"Wonderful!" Lily threw her arms around him and kissed his cheek. "The south of France! Provence!"

Madame Finch grinned at him as she reached for her keyboard. "*Bon voyage,* you two. Lily, I am only a phone call away." Jacques could have sworn he heard an evil-sounding chuckle as she terminated the web call.

Lily still had her arms around his neck, her smooth bare legs rubbing his, her thighs firm and tanned as her short skirt had crept up. "I can't believe it—this is so exciting."

He had to agree. Exciting, but damned inconvenient that his libido had come roaring back after being comatose for so long. And he'd promised to take the sexiest woman he'd met in years to the most romantic place on earth— and treat her as a sister.

Lovely. Lovely Lily, with sparkling green eyes and glossy peach lips begging for him to kiss them. For him to pull her into his lap and show her what real French kissing was about. But…no.

He patted her wrist and waved to the waiter for their check. She dropped her arms awkwardly and he pushed her wineglass toward her. "A toast to our trip."

"Cheers." She tapped her glass to his again. "When do we leave?"

"If we take the TGV high-speed train, we can leave early tomorrow and be in Avignon in under four hours."

"Only four hours," she breathed. "I won't get a wink of sleep tonight."

Jack gave her a **dry** smile. Neither would he, but for a different reason.

5

LILY COULDN'T HELP gawking at the TGV train, luxurious with comfortable red-and-gray seats. The seating arrangement in their car consisted of one seat on one side of the aisle and two seats on the other. There was the option of facing each other over a small table, which was what Jack had chosen when he'd booked their last-minute tickets.

They were on the upper level. Jack had called it a duplex, but Lily thought it was more like a double-decker bus, only with a roof, of course.

Lily handed Jack her suitcase and he tucked it into the bins at the end of the car. She took her purse and laptop with her, figuring the rest of her luggage was safe enough.

Jack settled into his seat across from her and was looking drowsy as the train pulled from the station. Lily was too excited to sleep.

He yawned and closed his eyes as the train gathered speed, passing through the Parisian suburbs.

Lily gasped as the train emerged from a tunnel into the countryside. It didn't seem as if they were going about two hundred miles an hour—unless of course you looked directly at the trees and bushes close to the line. They were a green blur. "Look at that!" But he was sound asleep.

He really had overextended himself with that hike yesterday—no walk in the park for him. Typical man, refusing to admit any weakness.

Lily could sympathize. How many times had she put on the infamous stiff upper lip during a difficult situation? Sometimes best to grit your teeth and soldier on. But now wasn't the time for that. She opened her laptop and began making notes for an entry for their train trip.

After an hour or so, she decided to stretch her legs and stepped into the narrow aisle, nodding to a stylish young Frenchwoman who'd had the same idea. She found the restroom, bought a snack from the bar between first and second class and then made her way back. She was walking at almost two hundred miles an hour—and her old gym teacher said she was slow—ha!

Right before she got back to her seat, she passed the Frenchwoman again. "Excuse me," she said in English.

"Of course. American?"

"Of course," Lily parroted back to her, feeling a tinge of jealousy at the dark-haired woman's overall ease. Ease in English, ease in how her hair fell onto her shoulders, how her clothes were fashionable but comfortable. And how in the world did she keep linen pants from wrinkling on a train ride?

But Lily wanted to be a better person than that. "You have a lovely country."

"Thank you. I have been to New York. Parts of it are nice."

Damned by faint praise. "As are parts of Paris."

But her return crack went over the woman's head because she was staring at Jack. "Your lover is very handsome." She was right—not about the lover part, but about him being handsome. Jack did look particularly gorgeous, almost like a Renaissance painting of a sleeping shepherd boy with his pale skin and reddish-brown hair, which curled slightly around his ears and neck.

Lily's hackles rose and she gave her a tight smile. She was about to say he wasn't her lover, but then realized, why give Frenchie an opportunity? "He is, isn't he?" A little devil made her say, "And wonderful in the bedroom, as well. So inventive." She fought back a blush.

"Frenchmen usually are, unlike American men." *Touché*. But Lily wasn't about to defend the lovemaking abilities of her country's male population, especially since she pretty much agreed.

"But he looks familiar." The Frenchwoman wrinkled her perfect brow as she examined the sleeping Jack.

Nice try, sister, she'd heard that before. "I don't think so. Now if you would excuse me…" She slipped into her chair and deliberately opened her laptop, typing words like *skhjaldhfkjhioeurio* and *dkoiasuejndkjfioadioufi* in an attempt to look busy. She peered at her screen. Geez, the mess looked like a cross between Greek and Old Norse. She backspaced until the nonsense syllables were gone.

Jack had fortunately slept through her bragging on his sexual prowess. She didn't know what had made her do that.

Yes, she did. Her face started burning. She'd been wondering about his sexual prowess ever since he'd turned up sexy and clean-shaven and she'd accidentally rubbed her thigh all over his.

She quickly opened a new document and began a blog post on travelling the TGV—*Train à Grande Vitesse,* the Train of Great Speediness. Like most things, it sounded better in French.

Like her name, Lily. Your average flower that showed up every Easter at the grocery store, like it or not. But it sounded better in French—Lee-lee. And even Jack's full name, Jacques. Exotic and adventurous, or was she reminded of old Jacques Cousteau specials on the nature channel?

"Jacques," she whispered his name, just to hear it from her own mouth.

He bolted upright, his eyes wide and staring. *"Quoi? Qu'est-ce qu'il y a?"*

"Oh, my gosh, I'm so sorry." She grabbed his hand. "I didn't mean to wake you."

"What?" He turned to her, his eyes coming back into focus. "Are you all right?"

"Fine." She patted his hand. "Go back to sleep. We still have a couple hours left."

He rubbed the sleep from his eyes. "No, I'm awake now. I thought I heard someone calling me."

Cringe. "I was chatting with this woman. Maybe you overheard us."

"Maybe. Do you have anything to drink? My mouth is very dry." She passed him a water bottle and he drained it.

"I'll get another." He stood and stretched, his shoulders filling out his thin pale green cotton T-shirt. "Do you need anything?"

Yeah, a cold shower for her libido and a bar of soap to wash her mouth out for lying. But since those weren't options... "How about an orangeade?"

JACK STOOD IN a quiet corner of the train's bar, sipping his own orangeade as he checked his voice mail. Four frantic messages from his *maman,* despite the fact he'd called her after leaving to apologize again for the ruins of her well-meaning, if not well-thought-out, party. He'd made it clear he and Nadine were permanently over, but her romantic soul probably thought they'd had a lovers' tiff. Not one voice mail or text from Nadine. Good. She'd gotten his message, then.

A voicemail from Frank in Portugal and a text from George—who knew where George was? He was traveling frequently back and forth to New York to spend time with his fiancée, Renata, a wedding-dress designer who specialized in vintage styles. Apparently Stevie was wearing one of her creations, and that was how she and George had met.

He hadn't talked to his friends for several days and called Frank first. His friend's yelp of delight was a boost to his dysentery-shriveled ego. Good thing it hadn't shriveled anything else—he hoped.

"Jack, you jerk, don't you check your voice mails anymore?" Frank clucked. He always was a mother hen.

"Nice to talk to you too, *mon ami.*"

"Hold on, I'm talking to George on the other line. Let me see if I can conference call on this new phone of mine." A couple clicks later, the three of them were conversing as if they were all in the same café.

After reassuring his friends that he was not on death's doorstep any longer, he mentioned that he was on his way to Provence.

"Wonderful!" Frank enthused. He loved being in the country himself and disliked city life.

"A diet of that hearty peasant food will fatten you up in no time," George added.

"Nadine called me a peasant the other day," he admitted.

Frank made a choking sound and George groaned. "When did you see that *puttana?*" Not a nice Italian word, but unfortunately appropriate.

He quickly explained about the fiasco at his mother's house.

"You did the right thing to get out of town as soon as possible. I know girls like her. They think the entire country is a wasteland between Paris and Nice. She'll never follow you there," Frank reassured him.

"From your lips to God's ears," Jack replied, having learned that most appropriate plea from one of his Jewish friends in New York.

"Amen," George replied piously. "I have church on the mind, my friends. Stevie and her Teutonic knight have come up with a handful of possible dates, and we are all meeting with the Archbishop Wednesday."

"Already," Jack marveled.

George cleared his throat. "Stefania has a request for you and I promised to pass it along."

"Anything," he replied promptly.

"She has realized her wedding will bring much publicity and wants to use that for the benefit of others. Would you be willing to sell her part of your lavender crop to help make a commemorative perfume to sell for her charity?"

"Sell? I'll give her anything she wants." Jack thought out loud. "Much of the crop is already spoken for, but there are several fields available that would be perfect for her project. Madame Simone Laurent is the master perfumer of the House of Laurent. She would be thrilled to work with your sister. I will inform the farm manager about the lavender."

"Ah, is that still Jean-Claude?"

"Of course." Jean-Claude had worked for his father and had even been a young worker when Jack's grandfather had been alive.

"Stevie will be sure to come to Provence herself. She adores Jean-Claude and his wife."

"Yes, Marthe-Louise is still housekeeper there. She

loves having young women around whom she can teach how to cook all the Provençal favorites."

"Well, you'll have to get on the ball and bring her a young woman to teach."

Jack gave a wry smile. Standing in the crowded bar of the Paris-Avignon TGV wasn't the place to explain that he was indeed taking a young woman to Provence. Frank and George wouldn't understand a brief explanation. "When would I have the chance to meet a nice girl? I don't work as fast as you, George," he joked. George had met his fiancée one day and invited her to Italy the next.

Jack realized with a jolt that he had met Lily yesterday morning and invited her to Provence yesterday afternoon. That put him one up on George.

And he realized he wanted to get back to Lily. "Thank you for checking up on me, *mes amis*. I will be in touch over the lavender."

They said their goodbyes and Jack hung up. He dumped his empty orangeade bottle in the trash and carried a full one back to Lily. She was staring at her laptop, her honey-blond hair escaping her ponytail. Although she was typing with both hands, she clenched a pen between her teeth.

When she saw him, she looked up and smiled at him around the pen. She quickly spit it out and gave him a wry grin. "Old habit. I was an inveterate pencil chewer until I gave that up—too many splinters. But I still seem to write better this way. Strange, huh?"

He sat down across from her, charmed at her little quirk. "What are you writing?"

"My impressions of the TGV, a couple video clips I took with my phone. I hope to get some travel articles published from this trip. I've been publishing a few entries and photos on a blog."

"You're blogging?" Still leery of his run-in with the press, Jack was reluctant to be a feature.

She must have read his demeanor. "Oh, don't worry. I'm only publishing photos of the attractions and a couple of myself when I was able to find somebody to take my photo."

Lily would be a huge attraction for any blog, especially one with male readers. "I would like if you don't show me in those photos. The organization I work for does not like its workers to have online photo presences. It makes us more attractive to would-be kidnappers." It was true. As a French nobleman, he would be the jackpot for any ragtag band of outlaws who'd scraped up an automatic weapon.

He'd dodged the bullet so far but would have to see if his foray onto the social pages would make the aid directors nervous.

Her eyes widened. "My gosh, I never thought of how dangerous that would be. Don't worry, I won't show you. And I mentioned you briefly once but called you Pierre as a pseudonym."

"Pierre?" He chuckled. That actually *wasn't* one of his names. "That was my great-uncle's name. He lived down the road from us and was a true Provençal character."

"Really?"

"But of course. He had his own vineyard and made vats of incredibly strong wine. He also had several mangy-looking hound dogs and would go into the hills in the winter to look for truffles—not the chocolate kind, but the real truffle. A special, underground fungus that only dogs and pigs can sniff."

Lily nodded. "They are quite good shaved over pasta. I've always wanted to try the Italian white truffle, but those are terribly expensive, even more than the black."

Now, how did she know so much about truffles? Most

thought truffles were chocolate bonbons. And many did not care for their earthy, fungal scent and taste. "I've never tried the white truffle myself."

She grinned at him. "We'll save our money and chip in. Last I saw, they were about $10,000 per kilo."

He winced. "Ah, so expensive."

"I know." She tapped the back of his hand with the dry part of her pen. "Between me, a writer, and you, an aid worker, we would have to save for years."

Jack nodded. Part of that was true. He'd refused most of his salary and had donated it back to the aid organization, so he wasn't swimming in cash. His family was loaded, as the Americans liked to say, but most of that was tied up in real estate, farmland and the house in Paris. He had enough for his daily needs and never considered tapping into the long-term investments. God willing, he wouldn't be the last Comte de Brissard, and he didn't want to be known as the profligate count that flushed the family holdings down the loo. "You must have worked very hard to be able to come to France."

She laughed. "You don't know the half of it. My magnum opera include 'How to Potty-train Your Toddler in Ten Easy Steps,' 'Top Ten Organic Dog Food Brands' and 'Ten Historic Heroines of Philadelphia.'"

"I sense a theme."

"Magazine editors love articles with numbers in them, and ten is usually about right. It makes good cover copy."

The first article struck him. "Lily, what do you know about potty training? You do not have any children, do you?"

"Of course not. I researched online and talked to moms and a preschool teacher." She frowned at him. "And what would I be doing here all summer on my own? I'm not one of those upper-class mothers who leaves her children with the nanny and jaunts off to Europe. No, thanks." She made a sour face.

Jacques nodded. His own mother had often left him with not only his nanny but with Madame Finch and Bellamy when she wanted to travel. It was a typical situation for children of his class, as Lily had so succinctly explained.

He wondered where she had learned so much about the moneyed class, like black truffles and absentee mothering. Maybe from American movies and television. They were notable for their celebrity interest.

She tipped her head to the side. "You know, you bribed me with telling me about French scouting but never did get around to that. Time to pay up. I may sell a freelance article on this." She clicked on her laptop. "Okay, here's a new file for my notes. Now tell me the French version of the scouting pledge." She looked expectantly at him.

Jack couldn't decide whether to grin or groan. He was thinking the least noble thoughts possible at how her breasts curved under her peach-colored T-shirt and how her enthusiasm was a bright sunburst compared to all the cool, collected women he'd known. "Well, there are many scout organizations in France depending on religion and politics."

"Fascinating," she murmured, her lips parting and eyes widening. His breath sped up, as well. "Tell me more, Jack."

"On my honor," he muttered, remembering his promise to Madame Finch, the governess with the evil streak. He could practically hear her laughing all the way from London.

6

LILY RESTED HER head against the seat in the rental car. They had arrived in the amazing steel-and-glass Avignon train station in less than four hours as promised. It left Jack enough time to show her the famous bridge of Avignon that only extended halfway into the Rhône River due to strong currents as well as the beautiful stone Papal Palace that was the home of several popes during the 1300s.

While they were grabbing a couple sandwiches for a late lunch, Jack had noticed a sign on a public bulletin board that a nearby town was hosting a lavender harvest festival. "Do you want to go?"

"Sure."

He had consulted the board again. "There are several hotels and a hostel. It's not a huge festival, so we should be able to find a couple beds at the hostel."

"Sounds good." A quiver ran through her stomach at the word *beds.* She'd been imagining Jack in a bed since last night. He'd given her nothing more than a couple sidelong glances but she could tell he was interested in her, too.

It had been so long since her last relationship, and the mild spark she'd had with her ex-boyfriend was nothing compared to the fiery sizzle she felt with Jack. She hadn't come to France to jump in the sack with a Frenchman, and it probably would even be counterproductive to her writing efforts.

On the other hand, France was full of examples of artsy types who managed to combine sexual passion and their creations. Look at Van Gogh—no, not him. Creepy. Or the sculptor Rodin and his protégée Camille Claudel—but she wound up in a mental institute. There was a huge Rodin gallery in Philly and Lily remembered that poor woman's story well.

Um, there had to be a happy ending there. Unfortunately, all she could think of were the artists who would have benefited from modern pharmaceutical therapy and the writers and poets who drank too much absinthe, the notoriously strong liquor that was banned in France about a hundred years ago.

Was that a blog post? See, she could combine her writing work and thoughts of him. A veritable romantic multitasker. "Jack, have you ever drunk absinthe?"

"Ah, they call that the green fairy for its color and supposed effects on the mind." He went on to discuss the active herbal ingredients in absinthe while Lily scribbled rapidly. He finished, "But there is little evidence that it can cause hallucinations, and it's now for sale in France again."

She shook her head. "Geez, you know a lot about the medical side of it."

He grinned. "And yes, I have tried it, but I don't care for it. Licorice-flavored, you see." He wrinkled his nose.

"Not a fan of that?"

"No, I prefer sweet things." Was it her imagination or did his gaze flick down to her bare legs and then up to her breasts? He was subtle, though. If she hadn't been so tuned in to him, she never would have noticed.

"If only they made lavender liqueur…" she teased him, wondering if he had meant her when he'd talked about sweet things.

"They do."

"Okay, another blog post for me." She started making notes again.

"You'll have time for writing later." He touched her knee to get her attention and quickly drew his hand back. "I want you to look around now so you can truly see what you're writing about."

She wanted his hand back on her knee, but it was firmly gripping the steering wheel. Instead, she looked out the window at the scenery. They'd just climbed a hill and the world was spread out before them.

Provence was beautiful—as if using that word was even a smidgen bit adequate to describe the land and the air, a crisp quality fragrant with floral perfume. Even better than perfume, because the flowers were alive and growing, putting out their scent with every touch of the breeze.

"It looks just like the paintings," she told him. "I thought those flat orange-and-purple landscapes were stylistically flat. But that's the way it actually looks."

He smiled. "The orange fields are *épautre,* or spelt in English. An old, old grain from the wheat family. It's been grown together with lavender for hundreds of years."

"No wonder you wanted to get out of Paris. This is heaven compared to the city."

"I agree. I'm glad you like it. This area is kind of a purple triangle of lavender growing. It's bordered by the towns of Sault, Banon and Sederon. Different varieties are used for different products, but the best and most exclusive varieties have a special designation, like wine. We take our lavender very seriously here—it's even called *l'or bleu*—blue gold."

"I can see why."

There was a small gravel pull-off area and Jack stopped the car there without asking. She hopped out to take pictures of the panoramic valley below.

He stood next to the front tire and stared out at the fields. Mindful of his privacy, she took a picture of him from the back, only the back of his head visible.

But even that was interesting. She lowered the camera. "Do you have a birthmark there, Jack?"

He rubbed the nape of his neck. "I suppose you can see that now that my hair is shorter. Yes, it's what they call a stork bite. Babies often have them, but they often fade quickly—mine never did."

"And what shape is that?" She came closer to see, her breath ruffling the tender skin.

A shiver seemed to run through him, and she fought the crazy urge to kiss the small red spot.

When he spoke, his voice was scratchy and he had to clear his throat. "I've only seen it in a mirror, but it looks like a heart."

"How cute." She rubbed her thumb over it and he turned, grabbing her hand.

"Sensitive spot." He held her hand for a second and then let go.

Sensitive or arousing? Lily was getting aroused herself, imagining her mouth, her hands on his smooth skin, his strong fingers touching her in all sorts of sensitive spots.

"Enough photos?" He stood next to the driver's door, obviously ready to get moving.

"For now, but I have plenty of camera memory and the will to use it." She hopped in and he pulled out onto the road again.

"Provence is a photographer's dream. In the summer, you can't drive down a village street without seeing someone with a camera. Out in the country, not as much, but you still trip over backpackers and campers."

"Did you grow up near here?"

"Not too far. My father unfortunately passed away when I was young and my mother now lives in Paris."

She wrinkled her face in puzzlement. "Why didn't you stay with her when you were in Paris? Is her apartment too small for the both of you?"

"No, she has a large enough place for me to stay, but she had many guests and I wanted to get away from the noise."

"I can see that about you, Jack. You have a touch of the hermit about you."

He gave a startled laugh. "Hermit? But I am hardly ever alone in my line of work."

Lily smiled. "And that wears you down, doesn't it?"

Jack slowly nodded. "*Oui,* I suppose it does. Sometimes I would bribe my tentmates to go to the mess hall for an extra hour so I could be alone."

"And you came down here for some vine-ripened aromatherapy. All you have to do is open your window and you get a snootful of soothing lavender scent."

He laughed. "But Lily, this is not true lavender here. This is lavandin, a hybrid that is more suited to homemade candles and laundry soap. In fact, the word *lavender* comes from the Latin word 'to wash.' I will show you the true lavender, like I am showing you the true France."

"And I appreciate you doing this for me, Jack."

But he was already shaking his head. "No, no appreciation necessary for me. If you see the real country, your articles will be strong and authentic, better for your career."

"How nice." He was thinking of her writing career? That was even more touching. On one hand, she was an open book, but Jack was still a bit of a mystery. "What did your father do before he passed away?"

"Many things, but his favorite was working in the lavender fields. Everyone works all day, every day, until the harvest comes in and the lavender goes to the distillery."

"A lavender farmer?" Lily gasped in delight. "No wonder you know so much about it."

He gave her a rueful look. "I was not spared due to my tender age. As soon as I was useful, I was in the fields with the men. And before the age of cell phones, I was the messenger boy, running from the fields back to the house to get supplies, check the weather report and most importantly, learn when lunch would be ready. Harvesters eat *a lot*. Probably over four or five thousand calories a day because the lavender is picked by hand."

"Your mother must have been busy cooking for them."

He choked back a laugh and gave her an incredulous look. "My mother wasn't much of a cook. One of the other local women was in charge of meals. Even now, *Maman* prefers parties to farming."

"But this is lavender. It's not exactly pig farming. I've been out in the Pennsylvania Amish country and, believe me, there are much smellier farms there."

"And that was her favorite part of the lavender. Being *from* the farm, not on the farm. She could give gifts of lavender perfume or sachets and pretend she pressed the blossoms with her own hands."

Lily laughed. "Your mother sounds like..." She didn't want to mention growing up in the servants' quarters. It sounded so archaic, and she didn't know if Jack was as egalitarian as he seemed. Some of the French were firmly steeped in the class system and regarded upwardly mobile women as peasant upstarts. "She sounds like a woman my mother knew. She would hire the best party planners, caterers, florists, musicians for her party and then act as if she'd done all the cooking and decorating herself."

Lily herself had served at dozens of Mrs. Wyndham's high-powered functions where local celebrities and politicians were frequent guests. Her mother had often roped her into waitressing if the caterers needed an extra pair of hands. Talk about humiliating—serving hors d'oeuvres to your classmates' parents and cleaning up broken glass and spilled booze when they'd had too much to drink. Worst of all was when her classmates were invited and she had to serve them. She wished more than once that she could wear a wig and sunglasses to those parties.

"Parties here in Provence are more casual. As long as you have plenty of good food and wine, everyone is happy." He turned a corner leading down into the town and they quickly came to a standstill in traffic.

Lily looked around. "I thought you said this wasn't a huge festival. When was the last time you were here for it?"

He grimaced. "Ten years ago."

"Looks like the world has discovered your sleepy little village."

"I suppose they welcome the increased tourist money." But he didn't look thrilled about it.

"Of course. Everyone has to make a living."

Jack nodded. "And times can be hard when you depend solely on the land. Many people here live mostly on what they grow in the garden and hunt in the forests."

"That's the trendy thing to do now—eat locally. And you can't get much more local than your backyard."

"We French are well-known trendsetters." He laughed. "And wild rabbits and wild boar are delicious if cooked for several hours in red wine." He deftly negotiated the narrow cobblestone streets, avoiding pedestrians with a death wish and other cars intent on fulfilling their desires.

"That sounds wonderful. Maybe I could try that this week."

He shook his head. "Eating locally means eating in season, and those are traditional fall dishes. You would have to be here in October or November when the weather cools."

"I'll be long gone by then."

"Ah, yes." They both sat in silence as the cars in front of them inched along. "But since you are here now, you get to see the lavender." He spotted a parking slot and shoe-horned the rental car into it. Lily wouldn't have had the nerve to even try.

"That's true, but I bet every season has something wonderful to see."

"I think so, but of course I am a native son." He turned to smile at her. It was such a sweet smile that impulsively, she grabbed his right hand where it sat on his knee.

His smile faded but he immediately tightened his fingers around hers. "Lily, I am supposed to be a gentleman around you." His voice was low and gritty. "I would not break a promise to you or Madame Finch."

"You are a gentleman, but maybe I'm not much of a lady."

His breath hissed out in anger. "Don't say that about yourself. You are more of a lady than those born to the title."

"And how would you know about titled ladies?" she teased, leaning into him.

His amber brown eyes searched her face, his face taut as if he were in the middle of a great conflict. He seemed to come to a decision and sighed.

She was going to ask him if he were all right, but then he closed his eyes and lowered his mouth to hers.

Her breath caught in her throat as their lips touched. Her eyes fluttered shut and she practically swooned at the soft, gentle pressure of his mouth. He lightly pressed a kiss to her and then, realizing her eager response, deepened it so her mouth was open and moist under his.

Jack groaned in satisfaction, murmuring her name. She grew brave enough to flick the tender inner margins of his mouth with her tongue, and his fingers tightened almost painfully on hers.

He caught her tongue and sucked on it, and she cupped the back of his neck to keep him close. Her other hand slid up from where it rested on his knee to massage his thigh, the crisp hair tickling her fingers.

Jack dragged himself backward, his chest heaving. His glance fell to her breasts. Her diamond-hard nipples pressed against her thin bra and T-shirt. He raised his hand to cup her breast and then dropped it to his side as if he'd lost all his strength. "Ah, *mon dieu*. Lily…"

She muffled his mouth with her palm. "If you are about to apologize…well…" His hot breath against her tender skin made her almost forget what she was going to tell him and she panted a couple times before remembering. "Oh, yeah. Don't apologize, okay?"

He nodded and she started to pull her hand back, but not before his tongue flicked out to taste her. She yanked her hand back in surprise, not offense, and he gave her a dry smile. "You see, Lily? I am not much of a gentleman after all. You may want to get out of the car before I start the engine and drive us somewhere without an audience."

She actually wavered. If that was what he could accomplish in the front seat of a miniature car, imagine what he could do with some working room. But was she ready to hop into the backseat with him?

Her hesitation was enough to break the spell. "Get out, Lily. I'll follow you in a minute."

"But why..." She spotted the front of his shorts and understood why he needed some down time, so to speak. She opened the door and staggered out, not in much better shape herself.

She quickly put on her sunglasses to hide her dazed expression. *Now what, Lily?* Jump into bed with a guy she'd met the day before? Not her style, but then the whole getting-to-know-you routine hadn't worked much for her previously. And it wasn't the whole perfumed air, blue sky and beautiful scenery that was making him appear so sexy. He just *was*.

She had the feeling she'd find him as sexy if she'd met him in whatever jungle he usually lived in. Maybe that was what had saved him from being snapped up? And did she even know if he was snapped up or single?

Nope, and she needed to learn that before she made her decision. She leaned down. "Jack, I'll be right back."

"What?" He started to get out of the car but made a face and sat back down. Lily stifled a giggle. She'd never had such an effect on a man before and it made her feel powerful. Sexy.

She whipped around the corner of an old limestone building and pulled out her phone. The number was the newest she'd input. "Madame Finch, this is Lily. I have a question for you."

She asked her question and got the answer she'd wanted. Now all she needed to do was make her decision.

LILY LOOKED AROUND the perfume factory in wonder. The House of Laurent was housed in a historic building painted the color of ripe cantaloupe with white-shuttered windows. Jack had gone to the hostel around the corner to make a reservation for them for the night. Lily was relieved to put off her decision, for tonight at least.

For now, she was on the clock, so to speak. She couldn't very well come to Provence and not write about perfume, could she? She took several photos of the display of ancient perfume pots, delicate perfumed gloves that had been all the rage in a smellier society, and Art Deco French glass perfume vials and cut-crystal bottles that were works of art in themselves.

She'd been lucky enough to catch two spots on the English tour, but where was Jack? Not that he needed a tour in English, but she found herself wanting to share more and more with him.

They had gathered the group when a hand rested on her waist—he was back.

"Just in time." She smiled up at him. "What's with the hat?" He was wearing an olive-drab, military style sun hat pulled down practically to his eyebrows.

"This? The sun is very strong this time of year and I am a bit pale."

"Oh, true. I have my own sun hat, but it's in the car."

"We can get it after the tour if you'd like." He cleared his throat. "The hostel had two beds left—one in the male bunkroom and the other in the female. I reserved them for us."

"Ah. Good." Right? She tried to ignore her feeling of disappointment. The tour started right after that and Lily was swept away in note taking.

Jack leaned down to her, his brim bumping her head. "If you don't get all the details, ask me later. We learn much of this growing up in the area."

"Great." After that, she relaxed a bit and learned about

different methods of extracting the fragrant oils from plants, such as steam distillation, pressing the flowers into fats and more modern methods such as volatile solvents and pumping gases into the flowers to release the scent molecules. "Very high-tech, isn't it?" she murmured to him.

"Pah. If you have premium flowers, you don't need fancy methods."

"A purist, eh?"

"But of course. You should never settle for less than the highest quality in everything."

"That's a nice theory."

"But not practical?"

She shrugged. "My budget doesn't always allow for top of the line in everything."

"Very true. But a woman's perfume should be an indulgence, something that makes her feel wonderful." He gestured to a case with a frosted-glass bottle blown into the shape of a swan.

"I can see that." This would make a great blog post.

"She lifts the stopper and fragrance fills the air. It reminds her of the last time she wore it because scent is a powerful memory trigger. Did she meet her lover then? Is she meeting him tonight?"

There was that word again. *Lover.* Lily listened to him, spellbound. His mellow baritone voice and his sexy French accent were hypnotic.

He continued, "Then she strokes the stopper over her neck, her throat, the hollows behind her ears, as she wonders what new memory she will make tonight."

"Um, wow." She cleared her throat.

"That is the magic of perfume."

She stared up at him, trying not to pant. "What perfume is your favorite?"

He leaned down to whisper in her ear. "Yours."

"But…but I'm not wearing any."

"I know." His breath feathered over her neck, sending a million nerve endings abuzzing. "The most intoxicating perfume of all is the scent of a woman's skin. Even the most skilled *parfumier* cannot duplicate that."

And if a skilled perfume master could bottle Jack's sex appeal, it would be a bestseller. But then she'd have to share it with another million women, instead of guarding it all for herself.

Lily smiled up at him. Maybe not tonight in the hostel, but soon, she'd open the bottle and make some new memories.

LILY COULDN'T BELIEVE how fast the day passed. A visit to the perfume lab, filled with pristine white furnishings and brown glass scent bottles, a leisurely lunch at a sunny sidewalk table and then walking around the town hand in hand so as not to get separated in the crowd—or so Jack claimed.

He could claim whatever he wanted as long as she could keep his strong fingers wrapped around hers. He showed her many of the historic buildings, including an ancient church, a historically accurate restored lavender press and an ancient plane tree that shaded benches in the town square.

Twilight was starting to fall, the pinkish-purple light bathing them in a rosy glow. Lily was tired from the sun and wine, but her nerves felt almost raw and jittery. She took some deep breaths. Tonight they would stay in the hostel and tomorrow was another day, as Scarlett O'Hara was wont to say.

She muffled a yawn with her free hand and rolled her neck.

"Tired?" He moved behind her and started rubbing her shoulders.

She moaned at the exquisite sensation. "Oh, yes, Jack. Harder, harder."

His fingers tightened and she realized how erotic she'd sounded. That wasn't far off the mark. She stepped away and turned around, not wanting to embarrass herself further. "Thanks, that felt great. What would you like to do for dinner? I have some granola bars and dried fruit in my backpack."

His pained expression made her laugh. "We will be able to find something more substantial than that." But after stopping in several restaurants around town where the crowds were standing-room-only and the wait for a table was hours, Jack was forced to admit defeat. "I suppose we could find something at the hostel, although packaged noodles and sandwiches isn't my first choice."

"Food snob." She handed him a granola bar, which he ate grudgingly on the way to the car to pick up their luggage.

The hostel was an old limestone building that looked suspiciously like a school. Jack confirmed her guess when she asked. "Yes, it was the local primary school for many years but the village built a bigger, more modern school at the edge of town. A couple years ago, an investor bought the property and had it remodeled into a hostel."

"Now we can legitimately sleep at school." He laughed as they went up the steps. "I feel like I should check in at the principal's office."

And the main office was now the front desk, the clerk a jolly older woman, unlike any principal that Lily had ever met. Jack greeted her and her face fell. She spread her arms wide and shrugged expressively, replying to his question.

Whatever they were talking about, it wasn't good news for them. His polite insistence didn't get him anywhere, only more expressive shrugs.

Lily touched his elbow. "What is it?"

He pursed his lips and puffed out a sigh. "She says when we didn't arrive in time, she gave the beds to someone else and now the hostel is full. They have no beds whatsoever due to the festival."

"So sorry, *mademoiselle*. But the clock…" She pointed at the utilitarian round black-and-white timepiece on the wall.

"Geez, where should we stay? Out in the park?" She didn't want to sleep out in the open but with Jack for company, it might be safe.

He conferred with the hostel manager again, who made a telephone call. "She's going to call one of the local women who has rooms for rent. Maybe she has something for us."

"Okay."

The hostel manager hung up the phone with a grin. "Ah, good luck *pour vous*. One chamber."

"Great!"

Jack got directions and they headed off. "It won't cost too much more than the hostel, and they might have breakfast for us."

"Really, I don't mind," she assured him. A pair of twin beds would be fine.

7

"Oн." Their impossible-to-find, last-one-available-in-the-whole-village room did not have twin beds, like every other European hotel room she'd ever heard of.

It had one single-and-a-half bed, because for sure that mattress was not a standard American double. Even that shrimp Napoleon and his wife would have barely fit in that sucker.

The rest of the room was pleasant enough with white walls and a small balcony overlooking the lavender fields.

Jack was chatting with the wizened madame who owned the house, who melted under his charms like a hot stick of butter. He turned back to Lily. "This is it, Lily. Can you make do?"

"Of course," she said brightly. "It looks…cozy."

He gave her a look that said he knew what she was thinking but made arrangements with the lady of the house.

Glad to be off the street for the night, Lily set her backpack on the floor and rolled her neck.

Lily couldn't help glancing at the bed. There was hardly anything else in the room. She suspected this had been either a poor relation's room or the maid's quarters once upon a time.

Jack cleared his throat and went to his backpack. "I'm going to take a shower. The bathroom is down the hall." He selected clean clothes and a towel and slipped into a pair of rubber flip-flops.

"Okay." Once he left Lily set up her laptop at the small desk and plugged in the round-pronged French electric adaptor. She selected several photos to upload from her camera to her blog and wrote several paragraphs about their arrival in Provence.

She stopped and realized that Jack featured prominently in her entry—what he'd eaten for lunch, what he'd liked best, how they'd found the last room in town...that had the smallest bed in France.

She dragged her eyes away from the bed and ruthlessly edited her rough draft. Readers didn't need to know everything. Jack was still "Pierre," a friendly Provençal local who had offered to show her around the perfume festival. She did add several of his insights on how the climate and weather was perfect for growing so many fragrant ingredients for the local perfumeries.

Her photos of the cut lavender in buckets looked great, and the elaborate glass perfume bottles from the antique store sparkled in the sun. If only the internet had smell-o-vision. But no shots of Jack's face online due to his request for safety reasons. She'd never asked his permission to post his photo and name.

She hit Post, and Jack was still safely anonymous.

And by the way, where was he? Surely done with his shower. A shower sounded like a good idea after hiking around the dry, dusty town, so Lily gathered her supplies and set off down the hall.

He wasn't in the bathroom, which was shoehorned into

a former broom closet by the looks of it. She'd take a picture later for her blog. No need for a wide-angle lens, that was for sure.

She took a quick shower to get the dust and sweat off and returned to their room. Still no Jack. Was he hiding until she was safely asleep? It was well past ten, but she wasn't tired at all.

Lily hadn't come to Provence to sit alone in her room. She went down the stairs and heard laughter coming from the patio. She poked her head outside and Jack was sitting in a comfortable looking wicker love seat, chatting with the plump lady of the household and her mustachioed, equally round husband.

Jack looked relaxed and cheerful, his hair slicked back from his shower and his towel and clothing folded neatly on the side table.

The older couple spotted her and beckoned her to join them. "Ah, *mademoiselle!*" the man exclaimed expansively, his mood no doubt helped by his big glass of wine. He struggled to his feet and eagerly shook her hand, planting a juicy smooch on each cheek. She was discovering that the people of Provence were avid hand-shakers in addition to cheek-kissers. One man in the flower market, his arms full of blooms, had offered his friend an elbow to shake.

Jack stood as well and greeted her a bit more coolly, still feeling the awkward vibe of too much bodyspace and not enough bedspace. He introduced Monsieur Roussel, the husband of the lady who was charging them an arm and a leg for the night.

Their hostess stood, as well. "Sit, sit." She pointed to the seat next to Jack and Lily sat. "Our wine." She poured Lily a big glass and went to a large stone table behind them, reappearing with two plates full of goodies.

"Oh, wow." Lily didn't normally eat so late at night, but when in France…

Madame Roussel spoke in an emphatic manner, waggling her finger at Jack several times.

"Is she chewing you out?"

"Yeah, Madame was horrified that we had granola bars for dinner and she thinks I am much too thin to be a proper Provençal—that's a man from Provence. The common physique is that of Monsieur Roussel."

"Ah." Lily nodded. Round, to be sure, but a more packed, prosperous fat, rather than flabby.

"Eat." Madame glared down at them.

Actually, Lily was hungry. The heat of the day had lowered her appetite, but now that the sun had set, she was getting it back.

She picked up a baby carrot pickled in vinegar and spices. The flavor was sour and fresh, crispy but mellowed around the edges by the vinegar. "Delicious."

Madame understood and beamed. *"Mangez, mangez."* She made a flapping gesture at the rest of the food.

"Eat up, Lily, we don't want to offend our good hosts."

"Of course not."

Madame pointed at Lily and said, "Tart."

Lily flinched. Was Madame some Provençal version of a gypsy mind reader?

Jack muffled a laugh. "It's a tomato tart. She's not making a comment on us sharing a bedroom. It would seem odd if we weren't."

"Oh." Now that she wasn't being scolded for wayward thoughts, Lily picked up a slice of tomato tart. It resembled a thin pizza with overlapping tomato slices. She bit into it and moaned in satisfaction. The pastry was crispy, almost like a puff pastry, and there was a hidden layer of soft, white cheese spread under the tomatoes. But the tomatoes were the star of the dish, thinly sliced and baked until chewy and almost caramelized around the edges.

Pure summer burst on her tongue, sweet and savory. "Oh my gosh, Jack, you have to try this. It is sooo good."

She shoved the tart between his lips and he opened his mouth in pure instinct. "Mmmph." He chewed and nodded in approval. Madame watched them both in satisfaction.

"Where does she get the tomatoes?"

Jack translated and their hostess laughed and gestured beyond the patio wall. "Her own garden, of course. The weather is perfect for vegetables of all kinds."

Lily cut another slice and handed it to Jack. "Eat." She sounded suspiciously like Madame.

"Bossy." But he took the tart and nibbled at it.

She finished hers quickly and moved onto a soft goat cheese spread onto a thin toasted slice of French bread. "Is this their own goat's milk, too?"

He asked and smiled. "No, the goats belong to Madame's brother."

"What a talented family."

Madame passed her a dish of what looked like olive spread. Lily spread it on another slice of bread and passed it to Jack.

"Trying to fatten me up?"

"Like a goose for *foie gras,*" she teased him.

Madame perked up. "Ah, *foie gras!* You like?"

Lily's mouth watered. "Oh, I love it, but I haven't had it in years." Mrs. Wyndham had served it at her parties, and Lily and the other staff snuck crackers full of it when they ducked back into the kitchen.

He looked at her in surprise. "You like *foie gras,* eh?"

"We have it in America, too." Especially if you'd grown up in the richest neighborhood in Philadelphia.

Madame disappeared into the house and emerged a

couple minutes later, triumphantly bearing a glass jar. She set it on the low table in front of them and unscrewed the lid with a flourish.

Lily leaned forward and gasped. Surely that huge jar wasn't what she thought.

"Pâté de foie gras!" their hostess announced.

"Holy cow, Jack, do you know how much a small jar of that stuff costs?"

He shook his head. "Homemade, probably from the geese of Madame's brother, along with the goat cheese." He listened to the older lady's explanation. "Ah. The geese belonged to her sister, and they were the plumpest, fattest geese in Provence."

"Mais oui. Très bon." That was the best French compliment she could manage, but it earned a wide smile.

And of course, after she had brought out the *foie gras* with as much pride as an American cook bringing out the Thanksgiving turkey, Lily couldn't refuse a hefty sample, along with another glass of rosé wine. Jack accepted a much smaller portion, and murmured, "That stuff packs a kick, Lily."

"What, the wine?"

"All of it."

She nodded, realizing her bare-bones, rolls-and-coffee Parisian diet was light years away from the food bonanza exploding in front of her. He was wise to eat in moderation, but her, she was perfectly healthy.

If the tomato tart was pure summer sunshine, the *foie gras* was pure autumn, earthy and dark. She'd never eaten it on a toasted baguette before, but it was the perfect combination.

Jack chatted with Monsieur and Madame Roussel as she sipped her wine and nibbled at the *foie gras*. Such a delicacy couldn't be gobbled.

He was careful to include her in their conversation, translating their recommendations for the tourist sites in the area and explaining the frequent bursts of laughter. Apparently the Provençaux were very fond of jokes.

She yawned. What a busy day. Closing her eyes, she leaned onto Jack's shoulder. He hesitated for a second but put his arm around her.

Did he smell good, his cologne a woodsy blend that fit this country setting perfectly. She snuggled into him, content to doze to the murmur of French voices and the drone of the cicadas in the trees.

She couldn't remember the last time she'd been so relaxed—replete with good food, good company and a good man. Jack was the best part, even better than homemade *foie gras*.

JACK RELAXED FOR the first time in a long time. He was finally home. He'd never met their hosts before, but they were still familiar to him, warm and hospitable and generous to a fault with the food.

That late-night snack had been more than enough to put anybody to sleep, but combined with heavy *pâté* and young wine that always had a higher alcohol content, it was a wonder Lily was still conscious.

And unless he wanted to carry her upstairs, he'd better get her to bed *immédiatement*.

Lily in his bed, warm and willing instead of stuffed and sleepy. The image was instant and powerful. He knew she would approach lovemaking with the same enthusiasm she approached life.

Ah, well, he'd given his word to be a gentleman, and gentlemen did not pour girls into bed and then crawl in after them for some nighttime sport.

He made his excuses and gave his thanks to the friendly couple. "Up we go, Lily."

She blinked at him with her big green eyes and extended a hand for him to pull her off the sofa. "Bedtime, Jack."

"Indeed." She wasn't intoxicated, just well-fed and slightly tipsy. He helped her up the stairs to their room and flipped on the light. The room was cozy and golden, the cream-colored embroidered quilt especially inviting.

He needed to decline that invitation. "Lily, you can have the bed. I'll sleep on the floor."

"What?" She wrinkled her nose. "Don't be silly. We can share the bed. I trust you."

He sighed. He didn't trust himself. "No, no, there are extra quilts and a pillow for me to use."

But Lily wouldn't take no for an answer. "You've had the same long day as I had, and you have even less padding for the floor. Don't be silly." She grabbed her toothbrush and left for the bathroom.

He stood in the middle of the room, at a loss. He'd thought he'd fallen into hell at his mother's party, but that was nothing compared to the hell of platonically sleeping with the sexiest woman he'd ever met.

Lily returned and crawled into bed, taking the side closest to the wall. "Don't be silly, Jack." She yawned. "Come to bed."

"I, uh, need to brush my teeth," he stammered.

"Hurry up. I'm beat."

He knew he was beaten too and shuffled to the bathroom. Staring grimly into the small mirror, he brushed the wine and *pâté* off his teeth.

God must be laughing at Dr. Jacques Montford, Comte de Brissard. He'd been arrogant enough to think he knew what was going to happen in his life, and boom! Illness hit.

He knew that happened, of course, but not to him. He was invincible. He fought illness for other people, not himself.

He sighed and spit into the sink. Ah, well. Like Lily had said, he was alive and it must be fate.

Walking down the hall, he considered the vagaries of fate. It was fate that he had literally bumped into her. And maybe it wouldn't be so bad trying to keep his hands off her.

He entered their room and stopped short. Lily lay sleeping on her back, the small bedside lamp gilding her hair and skin.

She was a golden angel, her plump lips slightly parted as her breasts rose and fell, the nipples poking against her thin cotton shirt.

With an effort, Jack dragged his gaze away and turned off the light. Crawling into bed, he perched himself on the far edge of the mattress and determinedly turned his back to Lily.

He'd promised to behave himself, even if it meant a long night for him. A long, hard night.

8

LILY DIDN'T WANT to wake up from her incredibly erotic dream. She'd never dreamed like this before, never dreamed of a man pushing his, well, erection against her bottom as he palmed her breast in his hot, rough hand.

She couldn't help herself and wiggled against her dream man, who was tall and lean with chestnut-brown hair. He responded by thumbing her nipple and kissing the back of her neck, his breath damp on her skin. She sighed at the wonderful sensations shooting between her legs. "Oh, Jack."

His hand tightened reflexively on her breast and her eyes flew open.

It wasn't a dream after all. It was Jack's hand on her breast and Jack's erection pressed between her cheeks. But only for a second.

He jumped out of bed like a horde of bedbugs had attacked him. "Ah, *merde,* Lily, I am so sorry." His distress showed up in his very French pronunciation of her name—*Lee-Lee*—with the emphasized second syllable.

Lily sat up and stared at the front of his short black boxer briefs. He was impressively aroused, the fabric doing little to contain his desire. But some guys got that way during the night. Maybe it didn't have anything to do with her. But he got larger as she watched. Maybe it *was* her?

He followed the path of her gaze and grabbed a pillow to cover himself. "Again, I am sorry. I should have taken the floor as we had discussed." He turned away and fumbled in his bag. "I have an extra sleeping bag liner. I will be fine."

"Jack." Her voice came out louder than she intended. He looked over his shoulder, startled.

She took a deep breath. "Do you want me?"

"I, uh…" He licked his lips, his breath speeding up.

That was enough answer for her. She slowly pulled her T-shirt over her head so she sat in bed wearing nothing but her boxer shorts. "Do you want me?" she repeated, growing in confidence.

"Yes…" The word was dragged from him, almost unwillingly. "God, yes…but—"

"What, Jack?" She got up on her knees to face him.

"I shouldn't, all right? You're a very sweet girl and I don't want to take advantage of you. Your first trip to France, and here we are thrown together in a small hotel room with the heat and the flowers and the feel of your skin…" He stopped suddenly, and that was when she knew she could have him.

And she wanted him.

She stood up and padded over to him. "What does my skin feel like?"

He stood there tongue-tied.

"Maybe you need to check it again." She shoved her boxers down and kicked them away so she was naked in front of him.

His hands twitched at his sides. She picked up his wrist and brought his hand to her hip. "How does my skin feel?" she repeated.

"Wonderful," he said hoarsely, his fingers tightening into her butt.

"More specific," she chided him, picking up his right hand. "How about up here?" This time she placed it on her breast.

"Like satin. Like silk. Like *crème*." He cupped her breast and stroked it gently.

"Like cream?" She was starting to breathe harder, his hands straying from their original positions. He kneaded her butt and he thumbed her nipple like he had while they were sleeping.

Only this time they were wide awake.

"I'll have to check to see if you taste like cream." He bent forward and nuzzled her neck. Lily clutched his shoulders as his tongue lapped at her skin.

"Well?" she managed to say.

"Better than cream. Cream with raspberries. Cream with honey." He stopped talking and did little swirls with the tip of his tongue.

"Ohhh." Her knees started shaking. "Jack, please."

"Please, what?" He laughed, his breath hot on her. It was a sound she hadn't heard from him before, pleased with himself and self-confident.

"You know." Heat climbed into her face, a mix of arousal and embarrassment.

"Tell me." He sank to his knees, sliding his mouth down her breast. He captured the peak between his lips, sucking it to aching fullness.

She gasped and ran her fingers through his thick, wavy hair. "Jack…"

"Mmm." The hum buzzed her nipple and she fought for balance, widening her stance. He cupped her butt in one hand, his other hand toying with the damp curls between her legs.

She fought for breath as he slipped his finger there, finding her moisture and spreading it up to her clit. A cry escaped her as he lingered there, massaging and rubbing the little nub. It had throbbed since he'd touched her in her sleep, creating that erotic dream that she had never wanted to end. "But it's not a dream anymore," she murmured.

He released her breast and rubbed his thumb over her slick nipple. "A dream come true."

She blinked hard at the sudden rush of emotion. He was right—she had never considered the possibility of finding someone like Jack, someone who could be her companion during the day and a powerful lover at night.

"Tell me what you like, *ma belle*," he continued conversationally, as if he were asking her how she took her coffee. "Do you like it slow and sweet?" He slowed his pace at her clit, dragging each caress out into a torturous pace. "Or do you like it hard and fast?" He flicked her until she fell back on the bed, her legs too weak to hold her up.

"I like it all. Any way you want."

"Good, because I have many, many ideas for you." He stretched out next to her. "Beautiful Lily. Such a beautiful woman. I fought to keep my hands off you, but sleeping next to you was too much temptation." He stroked her breasts and she arched into his touch.

"I knew it was you in my dream."

"Did you?" He toyed with her nipple, first one and then the other. "Have you been thinking of me that way?"

"I thought you were cute when we first met, but after you lost that shaggy look, you were gorgeous."

He puffed out a disbelieving breath. "I am not gorgeous."

"I am the only one in this room who is an expert on handsome men, so there. Unless you're putting on a phenomenal act..." she teased him.

"No act," he promised. "I have never been more sincere in my admiration."

She ran her fingers through the short chestnut hair on the nape of his neck and tugged his face down to her breast. "I'm in a mood to be admired, so keep going."

"Oh, you are a bold one." He kissed her breast but quickly moved right below her belly button.

Lily crimsoned in shock because she'd meant for him to keep going at her breast, not keep going down her body.

But he gently opened her folds, and at the first stroke of his finger all her protests dropped away. "Oh, Jack."

"Lily," he murmured. "Relax. Let me give you this pleasure." He guided her to sit on the edge of the bed and nestled between her thighs.

At the first gentle touch of his tongue, she cried out and he smiled against her. Her surrender spurred him on, as he slowly flicked her clit, then faster and faster until she fell back onto the bed.

Jack only stopped to hook her knees over his shoulders. In that wide-open, vulnerable position, Lily felt a moment of anxiety and closed her thighs around him.

He lifted his head immediately. "Are you all right, my Lily?"

His Lily. She liked the sound of that. And she liked how he made her feel—loved it, to tell the truth. She relaxed onto the tiny bed. "I feel wonderful."

"All right." He eased down again and in an instant she was lost in his touch. His mouth, his hands as they cupped her bottom, his cheeks as they brushed the sensitive inner skin of her thighs.

Her excitement started spiraling up into her belly and breasts, down her arms and legs. She tried pulling away again because it was too intense, but he held her close and refused to let her escape.

He seemed to know she couldn't take any more teasing and slipped a finger in and out of her slick, hot passage. She muffled a scream with her arm as he licked and stroked her. Her face burned and she could hardly breathe until he stopped and sucked her clit hard. She arched her back and climaxed hard, shaking with heat but shivering as if she had the chills.

Jack pushed her and pushed her until she couldn't tell where one climax ended and the next began. Finally she lay spent and limp under him and he stopped the exquisite torment, straightening to lie next to her.

He stroked her sweaty hair off her forehead.

"Wow. Oh, wow." She knew she had to look as if she'd run ten miles, but he didn't seem to mind. She smiled in an effort to stop panting.

He smiled back. "You liked that?" he asked eagerly.

"Very much." She caressed his cheek. "But what about you?" She tugged at his shoulders, encouraging him to move over her.

"Oh, Lily, Lily, I don't know how long I can last. It has been so long for me."

"How long?"

"Many months. Since long before I left for the typhoon and not since." He gave a quick grin. "Too ill to even consider it."

"You don't feel ill now." She ran her hand down his side, reveling in his lean masculinity.

"I've never been better." He grabbed her hand and pushed it aside. "But you have to let me prove it to you."

"Go ahead." She hooked her thumbs in his waistband and tugged. He twisted from side to side as they both stripped him naked, laughing as his underwear hit the floor.

She immediately grabbed his cock and he moaned. He

was long and thick, his silky skin covering a hot shaft. She brushed his fat tip with her thumb to spread his juices around.

"Ah!" He pulled away. "Not yet." He fumbled in his backpack and came out with a foil packet, quickly rolling on a condom.

Lily was disappointed because she hadn't gotten a good look at him in the dim light, but there would be many more chances to explore his body if she had her way. And it was time to have her way with him. She eased her thighs apart. "Come to me, Jack."

He moved between her knees and gently brushed her with his tip, wetting himself with her. He slowly slid inside as Lily consciously relaxed her internal muscles—it had been a long time for her, as well.

Finally he was locked deep within her and they both sighed in satisfaction. He felt wonderful, sure, but it seemed more than that. More as if he had claimed her, had taken her and said with his body, *She is mine.*

She blinked hard at her surprising sentimentality. He was a nice, sweet sexy guy, she was on summer vacation— the right mix for a fun holiday affair—no point in making it anything more.

"Lily?" he questioned gently, staring down at her. He could read her moods almost frighteningly well.

"Nothing." A rush of honesty prompted her to say, "I wasn't expecting this."

He smiled, shrugging as best as he could while bearing all of his weight on his arms. "I wasn't, either. But as you told me yesterday, I should look more to fate than to logic."

"Fate," she repeated. "But that means I'm not in control." And she hated that.

"Control is an illusion, a chimera. Life is a typhoon that

bears you where it will." He winked at her. "You will have much more fun if you lose control, especially tonight. I guarantee that."

She giggled. No more navel-gazing, especially since if she were to look down at her navel, she would see something infinitely more interesting than belly-button lint.

He started to thrust into her, and her giggles quickly turned to moans. She hooked her calves around his thighs, gripping his cock even tighter as she squeezed down on him.

Faster and faster he went, his butt and thigh muscles flexing. He dropped to his elbows, his chest hair catching and rubbing her nipples. She buried her face in the crook between his neck and shoulder, tasting his sweat. She had the most primitive urge to nip his skin—so she did.

He reared back in surprise.

"Did I hurt you?" How embarrassing.

A devilish grin spread over his angelic face. "My little cat has marked me. Did I taste good?"

She wiggled her eyebrows. "That part did. I'll let you know when I taste the rest of you."

His laugh turned into a groan and he lowered his head, slamming into her. "*Mon dieu,* the thought of your pink lips on me has tormented me all day."

Lily had a sudden fantasy of kneeling in front of him like he had kneeled to pleasure her. Sucking and caressing him with her lips and tongue until he exploded…she groaned and shivered.

"*Oui,* you want that, too. You are shaking around me." He leaned slightly to the side and slipped his fingers between them. "I'll make you shake even more."

He stroked her already swollen clit as he ground into her, his belly sliding over hers. His gaze burned dark and mysterious in the dim light. Heat built in her again, as if he'd never touched her before, never licked her to so many climaxes they all melted together.

But here it was again. He pinned her to the bed, claiming her. She wrapped her arms around his ribs and held tight. Her hips moved of their own accord, falling into pace with his rapid, almost frantic rhythm.

"Jack..." she gasped, desire boiling over. "I think I'm going to..." She gave up speaking and arched her back as an even more powerful orgasm hit, zinging up from where they joined into her whole body.

"Oh, Lily." He gritted his teeth and threw his head back, his neck pulling into cords. She held him tight as he jolted into her. Calling her name, he exploded, his cock jerking and pulsing deep inside her.

Slowly, he came down from his peak, panting as if he'd run all the way from Paris. He groaned and forced his gaze to focus on her. "Lily, are you all right?"

"Never better." She hugged him again and he sighed in satisfaction.

"Good. That is good." He slowly pulled out of her and looked around blearily. "Eh, this would be a good time to have a private bath."

She giggled. "You were the one who said Madame Roussel was much too sophisticated to shock."

He shook his head. "I am not worrying about shocking her—I am worried about being scolded for making a mess."

"How embarrassing."

He made do with several tissues and they tossed on some clothing. After they took turns sneaking down the hall to the bathroom, Jack urged her into bed. "You had your wicked way with me—now it's time for sleep."

"You were the one putting his hands all over me," she pointed out, taking off her T-shirt again. She wanted to feel his skin on hers, even if they were only sleeping. She slipped under the sheets, the cotton slightly more rumpled than before.

Jack shucked off his underwear. "You have a body made for pleasure. Soft and creamy-white in the moonlight, but with your skin you would be a golden goddess in the sunlight." He slid into bed next to her.

A delicious shiver rippled through her. "I've never been naked outdoors."

"Not even to sunbathe?"

She shook her head.

"Then not for sex."

"Nope again."

"We'll have to fix that."

"Outdoor sunbathing or outdoor sex?"

"Both." He swallowed hard. "And if that gives you erotic dreams again, please feel free to do to me whatever you'd like. I won't complain."

She yawned, utterly wrung out by their shockingly hot sexual romp. "Good. But let me catch up on a few hours' sleep first. By the way, how many condoms do you still have?"

He laughed and kissed the back of her neck. "Enough to last until the pharmacies open tomorrow." He wrapped his arm around her waist and she snuggled back against his warm, muscular chest. "Time to sleep, *chérie.* Tomorrow is a big day."

Oh, yes, it would be. Lily had big plans for hitting the sights—the sights of Jack, not the tourist kind.

9

LILY HAD SLEPT only until dawn. Jack was apparently an early riser in more ways than one. But she wasn't sleepy at all, thanks to the major endorphin buzz running through her veins. She and Jack making love…well, it was magical.

He came into their room as she was attempting to fix the nightmarish tangle of sheets that had once been neat and flat. They looked beyond hope. "Madame Roussel says our room is reserved for tonight and we need to find something else."

Lily straightened and nodded. The B and B room had been cozy but cramped, and the lack of connected bathroom was no fun. "You're the expert. Where's a good place to stay?"

He thought for a second. "There is a lavender farm up in the hills. My friend is the farm manager and I have stayed in the guesthouse before."

"Really? A lavender farm?" That sounded impossibly romantic.

"They are beginning the harvest, so it is a busy time, but Jean-Claude would not mind. What do you think?"

"It sounds wonderful, but I don't want to impose."

He waved a hand. "No imposition. Jean-Claude will be glad to see us."

"Well, okay." Lily began gathering her scattered belongings. "How far is it?"

"An hour or so, depending on traffic." Jack was much neater than she was and started rolling his clothing into tight rolls. "There is a nice pool and terrace with views of the fields. And a washing machine and dryer."

"Ooh, a washing machine?" That settled it. The bohemian life was fun, but dirty socks weren't part of the fun.

"Always practical, Lily?"

"Not always." She wiggled her eyebrows at him. "Flying to France alone and letting a sexy Frenchman sweet-talk me into his bed should qualify as extremely impractical."

"For the French, affairs of the heart are always practical," he informed her.

"Affairs of the heart—I like the sound of that. How do you say it in French?" She walked her fingers up his chest and curled them around the curve of his ear.

"Les affaires de coeur." He turned his face to nibble at her fingertips.

She leaned into his chest and cooed up at him. "Ooh la la."

He lowered his face to hers and captured her lips. She eagerly accepted his kiss, warm and affectionate, but playful and sweet.

A throat clearing from the hallway startled them apart. Madame Roussel eyed them knowingly and told Jack something.

His cheeks flushed. "She needs us to check out so she can clean the room." He bent to whisper, "And change the bedding."

Now it was Lily's turn to blush. She faced their hostess. *"Merci beaucoup,* Madame."

She waved a dismissive hand. *"Pas du tout, pas du tout."*

"Is that the same as *de rien?*" Lily asked Jack. He nodded. See, she was learning more French every day, although she'd bet several euros that several of the phrases he'd taught her last night were for bedroom use only.

JACK RELAXED KILOMETER by kilometer as they climbed into the rocky hills. Lily dozed in the seat next to him. He thought about pointing out some of the sights but decided there would be enough time for them to explore the outdoors later.

He glanced down at her. She was so beautiful lying next to him. He hadn't had the opportunity to watch her, except surreptitiously. He'd been right—she was a golden goddess in the pure sunlight, her honey-blond hair shining and her tanned skin glowing with good health.

The guesthouse he'd mentioned had actually been his uncle Pierre's house, an old farmhouse on the property. His uncle had decided to fix it up because it was far enough away from the main villa for privacy but close enough for the housekeeper to bring meals without the food getting cold. *Oncle* Pierre had been eminently practical.

The house had had the perfect setup for whatever sexual exploration he and Lily wanted—pool, hot tub, tiled terraces and a nice high wall around most of it to keep out prying eyes.

He knew she wouldn't be tanned all over thanks to her admitting she'd never sunbathed nude, but he was hoping he could convince her to try it with him.

He shifted in his seat as his cock hardened. Spreading coconut oil to slick her nipples and ass, their hot flesh sliding together as the sun beat down on them. He groaned and adjusted himself, but to little avail. The only thing better would be to take her without any barrier between them, his bare cock dipping into her tight wet depths. She would squeeze him, milk him dry as their juices mingled.

It was such a potent fantasy for him, the doctor who had never once in his disease-fearing life had unprotected sex. Dangerous, dirty and raunchy, but oh, so tempting.

He groaned again and forced himself to concentrate on his driving.

Lily opened her eyes sleepily and moved her seat upright. "You shouldn't let me sleep when I want to see the sights," she complained, rubbing her eyes. To his chagrin, her gaze fell on Jack's lap. "My, that is a sight." Her lips pulled back in a sly grin. "How long have you been driving around like *that?*"

"Not very long," he muttered. "Oh, look at that old barn." He was trying to distract her with the ancient building. It had been abandoned for years, and the scrub bush was starting to overtake it.

Lily glanced out the window. "Interesting. Can we see it up close?"

"We're almost to the lavender farm, and that is much more interesting." He needed to get her naked in that big four-poster bed in the master bedroom.

"No, no. This looks great. I want to take some pictures."

He'd distracted her too well. He sighed and pulled off the road, circling the bumpy road to the back of the barn. It was the typical creamy limestone found in almost every building. He cut the engine and undid his seat belt, but before he could get out, Lily's hand was on his lap.

He looked at her, startled. She smiled at him. "I think I found something more interesting than an old barn." She slowly undid his belt and zipper, and he bulged through the new opening.

She stroked the tight fabric over his erection as he stared

dumbly at her. "What were you thinking as you were driving?"

"What?" He couldn't remember what he'd been thinking as her fingers traced his shaft.

"Driving. Erection. You. And me, I hope."

"Of course. You, naked and slick in the sun."

"Mmm," she hummed approvingly. "What else?"

He shook his head. He didn't want to frighten her or make her distrust him with his fantasy of unprotected sex.

"Must be something really naughty." She shook her head. "You'll tell me sooner or later. Lean your seat back."

"No, Lily," he protested, but she pulled his briefs down and he jutted into the narrow space between his belly and steering wheel.

She traced a finger over his tip. "Now, how am I supposed to suck on you when I can't even reach you?"

He groaned and reclined the seat, a flush of needy embarrassment climbing his face.

She laughed softly. "Oh, Jack, so shy?"

"No," he choked out.

"Good." She gently kissed his tip. "I've wanted to do this since last night. I didn't get a good look at you."

"And what do you think?"

"Very nice." She cupped his shaft and played with the head. "You really want me, don't you?"

He brushed his thumb over her cheek. "What gave you that idea?"

"I'm a good guesser," she teased him.

"No guessing needed. You ask me and I'll tell you the truth." At least part of it.

She smiled and gently blew on him.

"Ah, Lily." He threaded his fingers down to her scalp, pulling out the band holding her hair back. The golden brown mass fell over her rosy cheeks and brushed his groin.

She enveloped him with her mouth and he clenched her hair. She was wet and warm around him, like last night. He thrust up between her lips.

It was heavenly. Lily was heavenly. She sucked deeply on him, jolting his nerves from head to toe. He dug his heels into the floormat, her hair wrapping around his hand.

She gave an utterly feminine hum of satisfaction, the vibration buzzing his shaft. Sweat beaded on his forehead and dampened his shirt. She swirled her tongue around the head of his cock and then licked him from the base to the tip as if he were an ice-cream cone.

His balls tightened and he gasped in pleasure. He'd never been so decadent, so intoxicated with lust, the southern sun burning him from the outside as Lily burned him from within. The cicadas buzzed and blood pounded in his ears. "Ah, Lily," he moaned. "Stop, stop. I'm losing control."

She laughed and lifted her mouth for a second. "Good, that's the idea." She resumed her tender caresses and sucked him deep.

He couldn't hold back any longer and exploded, Lily draining him dry until he stopped bucking and jerking under her.

She finally lifted her head and smiled at him. "Jack."

He stroked her silky hair down to the nape of her neck, amazed at her sexiness and sheer generosity. "Lily, you didn't have to do that—I never expected you—"

"I know." She smiled mischievously at him. "I'm learning to expect the unexpected this whole trip. But it was all my idea and I really wanted to pleasure you like you did for me last night."

"Thank you, Lily." He pulled her into his arms and hugged her.

She shook her head. "No thanking allowed. Unless you want me to start thanking you for everything you've done."

"No." He didn't want gratitude from her. "I want your warmth, your passion and the pleasure of your company. Gratitude is not on that list."

"That sounds lovely. You're lovely." She smiled at him and his heart flipped.

"Don't be silly," he said gruffly, trying to cover up his unruly emotions. "Men aren't lovely."

"You are." She kissed him on the cheek. "Can you show me around the barn?"

Jack laughed and fixed his clothes. "Back to work, eh?"

"A freelancer is never off the job." She started to blush. "Except for certain occasions."

"Exactly." She charmed him with her mix of boldness and shyness. He hopped out of the car and helped her out of the other side, where she oohed and aahed over the typically Provençal building.

Jack smiled to himself. If she liked this old wreck, she'd fall in love with the estate's guesthouse. And he'd love seeing her there.

FORTUNATELY FOR LILY, there was plenty on the drive to distract her from memories of her boldness. She'd never imagined she'd do *that* to a man in a parked car, but she couldn't help herself. Seducing Jack was as intoxicating as the local wine, and much more fun.

It was so flattering to know that watching her sleep aroused him to a fever pitch. And to feel him under her mouth—wow. It had been incredibly arousing and she couldn't stop thinking about the next time they would make love.

She knew it was just a vacation fling, but sex with Jack was more than scratching an itch—she was glad to be with him and get to know him in and out of bed.

Did the house he had mentioned have a nice bed? Anything would be better than the tiny one they'd shared last night, but they had managed just fine.

"Almost there." Jack turned down a narrow unpaved lane saved only from tedium by a row of trees on each side. Their trunks were silvery-white and mottled, almost as if some avant-garde artist had sculpted them out of concrete and then sandblasted them to make them look old. The branches grew straight up with glossy green leaves.

"What kind of trees are these?"

He slowed the car to avoid kicking up dust. "Ah, plane trees—from what you call the sycamore family. These are very old and have been trained over the years to grow upward, unlike the ones in the village that grow horizontally."

"Mmm." Lily pointed her camera out the window and took several shots. It was like driving in a green, leafy tunnel, much nicer than the New York underground version. Then the tunnel opened up on a stunning view of a gigantic stone manor house with a fence surrounding it. Lavender fields grew in the distance, their purple rows stunning alongside the low-growing orange spelt crop. "Holy cow, Jack. Whose house is that?"

He smiled at the building. "Isn't it beautiful? It's been here several hundred years and the owners have enlarged it over the centuries."

"This is your friend's house, then. What's their name?"

"The de Brissard family owns it." He shifted in the seat. "The guesthouse is another couple kilometers down the road and past that are the lavender fields and the farm buildings. There is even an old lavender press dating from the early Middle Ages. The farm, however, now uses a more modern facility in a nearby town."

"Hygiene and regulations suck the romance out of everything." She shook her head. "And I suppose you can't have the peasants crush grapes with their feet anymore, either."

He laughed. "Not unless you want to make the bureaucrats faint from horror."

They passed the main house and Lily craned her neck. "Can I have a tour of the mansion sometime? I'd love to see the inside."

"The housekeeper would love to give you one. They are very busy this time of year with the beginning of the lavender harvest. Many migrant workers come and Marthe-Louise and her staff make sure they all have enough to eat and drink. We keep the best workers that way."

"Oh. But if they're so busy, they might not want us borrowing the guesthouse."

"No, nobody is using it now and we are well out of the way of their work."

"If you're sure…"

"I am positive," he said firmly. "Please do not worry that you are imposing because that is not the case. I would never put you into an awkward situation where you are not welcome."

"Thank you, Jack." She couldn't reach him to kiss his cheek, so she patted his knee.

He smiled at her, his warm, relaxed smile that was appearing more and more frequently as they settled into Provence. "You are most welcome." He covered her hand with his and steered around a corner with his left hand. "And here we are."

Lily gaped at the guesthouse. It was smaller than the

main house but no less impressive. Jack parked the car in the circular gravel driveway next to a limestone fountain. She hopped out to admire the two-story stucco building. It was a lovely weathered peach blush color with pale blue shutters and white trimmed doors. The roof was Spanish-style red clay rounded tiles. She guessed it was too dry to grow a traditional American lawn since the grounds were landscaped in beds of carpet-type junipers, silvery hedges and tall evergreens pruned into perfect slim columns.

"This is called *la petite maison*—the little house."

"Little? How many bedrooms?" Her shoes crunched on the pure white gravel as she approached the fountain.

He hopped out of the driver's seat and looked up at the house. "Four, five if you consider the den has a sofa with a pullout bed."

"Oh, only five bedrooms—a real hovel." She twisted her camera strap. "Jack, this is too much. We can't just show up, even if they are your good friends."

He caught her shoulders and kissed her forehead. "Would it make you feel better if I called the farm manager and talked with him first?"

"Yes." She smiled in relief. She had no desire to do firsthand research on what the local French police did to trespassers. Not exactly good blog material.

"Good." He reached into the backseat and pulled out a water bottle. "Here, have a drink while I call Jean-Claude. I'm going to walk down toward the main house where the signal is better."

Lily nodded and unscrewed the bottle. Jack flipped open his phone and gave her a reassuring smile as he walked down the driveway.

She turned to look up at the guesthouse—the "little house." It would be wonderful to stay there, a luxurious hideaway of all the best of Provence.

Undoubtedly there was a beautiful garden in the back and killer views. But the best part would be spending time with Jack, to explore its four bedrooms with him. Five, if they considered the den, but Lily didn't expect a sleeper couch mattress would be all that comfortable.

She sighed. Maybe she was getting in over her head. Anybody would be. A chance meeting two days ago with a sexy Frenchman, a trip to Provence, unexpected passion last night and the prospect of even more in idyllic settings would turn any red-blooded American woman's head.

Lily would have to be careful to keep a good head on her shoulders. She was a writer in search of interesting stories, not a sappy tourist who, disillusioned with American men, had come to Europe in search of "true love."

And was it possible to be disillusioned if you had few illusions in the first place?

10

Jack waited until he was out of Lily's hearing and called Jean-Claude, his estate manager. Jean-Claude was not merely an employee, but more like an uncle. He had taken Jack under his wing after Jack's father died. Jack's mother was a sweet lady—too sweet-natured to deal with the precocious, obnoxious boy he'd been. Fortunately for Jack, Jean-Claude and Madame Finch were not sweet-natured in the least.

"Allô?"

Jack couldn't help but smile at the familiar sound of his old friend's heavy Provençal accent. "Jean-Claude, *c'est moi*—Jacques."

"Jacques? Where the hell are you?"

"Shhh. Meet me in down by the old oak tree near the fence line."

"You're here?" he bellowed.

"Calme-toi, mon ami. I will tell you everything as soon as you get here."

Jean-Claude grunted and hung up. Ten minutes later the sturdy man was standing on his toes so he could shake his finger in Jack's face. "And you are back in Provence after nearly dying in whatever jungle hellhole you ran off to, and you expect me to come running? We happen to be in the middle of the lavender harvest, in case you've forgotten. Lavender that I am harvesting for you, *M'sieu le Comte.*" He pursed his lips and then grabbed Jack for an emotional embrace. Jack got kissed on both cheeks and then once more for good measure.

Jack patted Jean-Claude's back, accepting the traditional French greeting. His estate manager had probably received a hysterical phone call from Jack's mother describing his admittedly nasty case of dysentery as a cross between the bubonic plague and Ebola hemorrhagic fever. "Eh, *mon vieux,* as you can see, I am here and healthy."

"*Bien oui,* you are too skinny." Jean-Claude released him, the corners of his sun-creased brown eyes crinkling as he gave him a hard stare.

Jack shrugged. "A few kilos, that's all."

"More like ten." Jean-Claude sniffed. "And now that you are here, you will stay with us and Marthe-Louise will cook for you all your favorites." Marthe-Louise was the family cook and also Jean-Claude's wife.

"Actually I'm not staying at the big house." He braced himself for the explosion, which erupted right on schedule.

"You come here sick and skinny and then you tell me you will go?" Jean-Claude gestured voluminously. "Go where? Go fall down in the lavender field and die? Eh, we could use goat shit for fertilizer—you do not need to volunteer!"

"Jean-Claude, *s'il te plaît,*" Jack soothed. "I called you because I can trust you." He lowered his voice and looked around the empty courtyard like a bad dinner-theatre actor. "It involves a woman. A special woman."

"Ah!" His old friend burst into laughter. All was forgiven if women and sex were involved. "Why didn't you say so?" He dug his elbow in Jack's side with less force than usual. "And this woman, where is she?"

"Waiting at the little house."

"La petite maison? Why?"

Jack knew this next part would be the trickiest. "She doesn't know I own all this. I don't think she likes rich guys."

Now Jean-Claude was really laughing. "Pull the other leg, Jacques. What woman doesn't like rich men? Or is she not very bright?"

Jack made a chopping gesture with his hand. "Enough." Jean-Claude raised his bushy eyebrows. Jack hardly ever used his aristocratic mien. He continued, "We will be staying at the *petite maison* and I do not want her to know the extent of my holdings. She is an independent American girl and very much believes our French concept of *liberté, fraternité* and *egalité.*"

Jean-Claude gave a loud snort. He knew himself the equal of any man in France, but knew the class system had well survived the Revolution. "If you say so, milord."

Jack rolled his eyes. "If you're going to act the role of a peasant, at least give a little bow or avert your eyes as you talk to me. Now as you know, Princess Stefania will be setting her wedding date soon, and she needs lavender oil for a special perfume. She is planning to sell it for the benefit of her children's charity. Do we have enough high-quality lavender to supply her needs?"

Jean-Claude drew himself up in affront, as if explaining their business to a particularly dim-witted farmhand. *"M'sieu le Comte,* all our fields are, *as always,* Haute-Provence Lavender, designated by the government as AOC, Controlled Destination of Origin. We *never* have low-quality lavender." His lips curled at the very thought, and he spit on the dry ground.

"Very good." He wrapped his arm around his friend's shoulders. "Where would I be without you, *mon vieux?*"

Jean-Claude puffed out his lips. "Taking care of your own land and your own lavender."

"I know, I know." Jack raised his hands in surrender. "But I am still grateful. And Princess Stefania will be, too."

"A wedding for her. I remember when she came for the summer when she was what, twelve? Thirteen?"

Jack nodded.

"Marthe-Louise taught her how to cook, how to garden, how to sew. My poor wife, she cried for weeks when Stefania left to go back to school."

"I'm sure Stefania will want to invite both of you to her wedding."

Jean-Claude shuffled his feet and looked at the ground. "Eh, why would she want two old Provençal peasants at her fancy wedding? Us rubbing elbows with all the aristos and royalty in Europe."

"Marthe-Louise would chase you with her carving knife if you declined the invitation and you know it."

"*Eh, bien,* you are right, Jacques." He heaved a theatrical sigh. "If we are invited, I suppose I must buy Marthe-Louise a new dress."

"Probably two or three," Jack pointed out. "And a new suit for yourself." He happened to know that Jean-Claude's good suit was a relic from Jack's parents' own wedding, more than thirty years ago. The lapels were wide enough for Jean-Claude to hang glide off the mountains of the nearby Haute-Alpes.

The older man winced. "Well, for Stefania, I will do it."

"Good man." Jack clapped him on the back. "I am not sure how long Lily and I will be staying, but if Marthe-

Louise wouldn't mind cooking an occasional meal for us…"

"She is away in Nice with our daughter who had a baby but will be back in a couple days. And what did you say? This girl's name is Lily?"

"Yes, why?" he asked, unsure why Jean-Claude was fighting a smile.

"Ah, ah, ah." Jean-Claude wiggled his gnarled finger at Jack. "You be careful, *mon ami*. This girl is already part of your life."

"What? Why do you say that?"

He lifted his hand in mock innocence. "Because of the de Brissard coat of arms, of course. A triple *fleur-de-lis* on a red background—three lily flowers. *C'est parfait*— it's perfect!" He doubled over in laughter as Jack realized his friend was correct.

For the past thousand years, the family's coat of arms had been golden lilies on a red shield. He'd grown up seeing them every day but had never thought much about them.

Now he had his own Golden Lily. But how could she be a part of his life? And did she even want to be?

LILY WANDERED AROUND the courtyard, wondering what the fountain looked like with the water turned on. It made sense that it had been shut down if there was no one staying there. A working farm had priorities for water elsewhere, especially if they were irrigating vegetables or flower crops.

She sat on a bench in front of the house and wondered if the house's blue shutters were decorative or functional. Probably both, considering what she'd read about the wild mistral winds that funneled south from the mountains.

Fruit trees lined the courtyard—always practical, those

Provence farmers. Almond, apple, cherry and dark plum. Ooh, and a fig tree. You didn't see those outdoors in Philly, and this was a big fig, its grayish trunk a mass of columns as if it were many tree trunks woven and grown together.

The still, warm air buzzed with the sound of cicadas. It was as if she had fallen back one century, even two, as she sat in the quiet courtyard.

And this was Jack's country. No wonder he had looked ill at ease in noisy, gray Paris. He thrived on warmth. Warm sun, warm people and warm colors.

She was flowering as well in Provence, enjoying the beautiful scenery and kind people. But Jack was the biggest reason she was enjoying herself.

Lily leaned her head back against the thick plastered wall and closed her eyes. Yep, she could get to like this too much. She must have dozed off because the next thing she realized, Jack slid next to her on the bench and kissed her awake.

"Hello, Sleeping Beauty."

"I'm no beauty."

He laughed and then grew serious when she lifted an eyebrow at him. "And you think you are not?"

She shrugged, uncomfortable at this serious turn of conversation. "I'm not particularly blonde, particularly tall or particularly, um, well-built."

"You have hair like honey." He cupped her jaw and lifted several strands. "It shines golden-brown in the sun. You are the right height to fit against me. And if you were any more shapely, I would be an even bigger gibbering idiot when you are near me."

"You don't seem like an idiot now."

"I hide it well." He brushed her hair to the side and kissed her cheek. "All I want to do is stare at you—and try not to drool down my chin."

She gave a startled laugh at the image of sophisticated, urbane Jack with drool down his chin because of her.

"And you are even more beautiful when you laugh."

"Really?"

"Really. Now come see the house. I talked with Jean-Claude and he was happy to let us stay here."

"If you're sure."

"Positive." He selected a key from his ring and unlocked the front door. "Come see. I think you will like it."

Jack pushed open the door and ushered her in. She stood there enjoying the sunny, two-story entryway while he carried in their bags. "*Voilà*, the foyer." It was a wide, modern-size space with a sweeping staircase going up into the second floor, but the bones of the house were definitely not modern. The exposed walls were old limestone like the outside, and the ceiling was white plaster with dark timbered crossbeams that were obviously not only decorative but still structural.

"How old is this place?" It looked even older than Mrs. Wyndham's house, and Ben Franklin had actually dined there with a Wyndham ancestor.

"It was an ancient farmhouse that *Oncle* Pierre renovated, adding all the modern comforts, of course. This main level used to be the stable, and the heat of the animals would rise to the rather meager living quarters upstairs. It is of course several times larger than it used to be."

"*Oncle* Pierre?"

"Yes, he was the younger brother of the family. Wanted his privacy." Jack shrugged matter-of-factly. "His mistress was not only a very famous actress, but a married one, no less. They needed much privacy for their rendezvous."

Lily pursed her lips and Jack laughed. "Do not worry about that lady's husband, *chérie*. He had a boyfriend of his own. Everyone was very civilized, and I believe they used to exchange Christmas presents."

"Hmmph."

"Ah." He carried their luggage up the front staircase, framed by an elegant wrought iron railing decorated with bronze medallions of bundles of lavender.

"What do you mean, 'ah'?" Lily narrowed her eyes at his back.

He pushed open the door to a wide, airy bedroom. It had a large bed with four dark wooden posts rising to a canopy frame. Gauzy white fabric draped artfully from one side to the next. "You are worried that I am very civilized, that I have a wife or mistress—or both, and they are all very French and unconcerned about my doings. Is that right?"

"Madame Finch said you didn't," she muttered.

"Madame Finch?" His eyebrows shot up. "When did you ask her about my sex life?"

"I called her after you kissed me in the car. She says you are single."

"And did she ask why you wanted to know?"

"I told her you'd just stuck your tongue in my mouth and I needed to decide whether or not to have sex with you."

He made a small choking sound.

"Because I really, really wanted to have sex with you, but I wouldn't if you were involved with someone else. She gave me the all-clear and said to have my wicked way with you."

"That does sound like something she would say," he replied dryly.

She couldn't keep up the joke any longer and giggled. "Oh, Jacky, don't be silly. I asked her about the being single part. We were very civilized, as you say."

He set down their backpacks on the wide wooden planks

of the floor. "I can tell you I have no wife, no fiancée and no mistress. I am normally a very orderly, very civilized man, but I have found over the past day that that veneer of civilization is paper-thin and peeling off me as we speak." He yanked off his T-shirt and tossed it away. He unlaced his boots and kicked them and his socks free. "And I like it very much when you call me 'Jacky.' Maybe you can call me that when I am pounding inside you."

Lily's jaw dropped as Jack dropped his shorts and briefs and stood entirely naked in front of her. "You don't look civilized at all."

"Good. Now take off those clothes before I rip them off you." His eyes glittered, and she knew he meant it.

He looked primitive and aroused, his cock jutting up into his belly, huge and dark with blood, a drop of silvery moisture slicking his tip. His heavy sac rested on a nest of dark brown hair and a vein pulsed along the side of his shaft. An answering throbbing started between her thighs. She had never seen him totally naked in the daylight, and he was impressively built. A little thin, but still muscled, his shoulders broad and tapering into a narrow waist and strong thighs.

He pulled a foil packet out of his backpack and covered himself. No pretending with this man. He knew she wanted him, and he wanted her, too.

Of all the stylish, sophisticated women in France, he had chosen her. And she had chosen him. She slowly pulled her shirt over her head and ditched the rest of her clothing until she stood in front of him in her plain cotton bra and matching panties.

"Take it all off." A command, not a suggestion.

Her underwear joined the rest of her clothing. She shivered under his hungry gaze.

"And you say you are not beautiful?" He shook his head.

"Mon dieu." He stalked toward her, his cock bobbing with each step. Lily waited in anticipation for him.

Jack scooped his hands into her hair and crushed her mouth to his. She gasped and he took advantage of it to plunge his tongue inside. He stroked her tongue with his, sucking on her and letting her suck on him.

Her breathing came fast and hard, and she clutched his wrists. Jack was right—he was being totally uncivilized and savage, and she loved it. He moved her backwards so the edge of the bed clipped her legs and they sprawled onto the bed in a tangle of limbs.

His thigh had come to rest between hers, muscled and hot on her clit. She automatically moved against him, and he smiled, slowly rubbing up and down so the hair rasped her tender folds. "You like this, eh?" He lowered his head and nibbled her neck.

Lily arched her back as his mouth traveled leisurely across her skin, licking and sucking her tender earlobe, down to her collarbone.

"Lovely Lily," Jack murmured. "You turn me into a savage. I want to suck on your golden skin, give you a love bite."

She shivered at his sultry tone. "Why would you do that?"

"To stake my claim on you. So every man who sees you knows that you are taken. Possessed. Mine."

"And what should I do so other women know you're taken?"

"Nothing. I do not even see other women since you have dazzled me so."

"Oh, Jack." She grabbed the sides of his head and brought his mouth up to hers.

He kissed her eagerly. "It's true, I swear," he explained between planting kisses on her cheeks and lips. "You may think we Frenchmen are casual about *l'amour,* but I am not. I never have been."

"Me, neither." Lily gasped as he moved down to her breasts. "Oh, Jack, that feels so good."

His only reply was a muffled hum as he sucked on her nipple, rubbing his thigh between hers. His cock swelled even more, rising to her belly.

She wrapped her hand around him and shifted so he was brushing her opening. "Come inside me, Jack."

He shook his head. "No, you need more."

She guided his hand between them. "Does this feel like I need more?" She was dripping wet and throbbing.

He gave her a slow smile. "Why, yes, it does. More of this." He slid a finger into her tight passage and she squeezed down on him. "More of this." He moved his finger in and out, rotating it around like a naughty little sex toy. He brushed a particular spot and she squealed in surprised pleasure. He immediately returned there. "Oh, yes, the G-spot. And yours is so sensitive. You must like coming from this."

She shook her head.

"You don't?" he asked in surprise. "Do you want me to stop?"

"No! I never have before."

His smile grew positively wicked. "Then allow me to be the first." He circled her G-spot and alternated light and firm pressure across it.

She gasped as he devoted his entire attention to those few centimeters of tender flesh, murmuring in French as he touched her. She almost came from listening to his dark, sexy accent. He could have been reciting French nursery rhymes for all she cared.

Then he switched into English. "Beautiful Lily, I love to see your naked breasts pointing up, waiting for me to suck on the hard tips. I love to see your smooth skin bead with sweat so I can lick it off. And I love stroking you inside, so wet and hot and tight that I wish it were my cock inside you instead of my finger."

Her nipples tightened even further at his raunchy sex talk and she grabbed at him to put his money where his finger was, so to speak.

"Not yet. I'll take you when I say so." He easily fended her off with an increase in speed that left her gasping.

It was a pleasure that spiraled upward, burrowing deep into her very center, a pleasure that skirted the edge of pain from its intensity. A pleasure that made her dig her heels into the soft bedding and arch her back off the bed as if she were a bow drawn taut and he was a master archer.

"That's it, Lily, beautiful Lily," he coaxed her. "Surrender to yourself. Surrender to *me*."

"No." She whipped her head back and forth. She wouldn't surrender to him or anyone.

"You want to," he whispered. "You want me to possess you. Like you possessed me with your wicked mouth in the car. Mindless, physical passion."

She groaned. She'd always been careful to have her mind rule her body, but Jack was turning everything upside down with a wiggle of his finger.

"Do it, Lily. Lust. Sex. All you have to do is feel."

Suddenly she was tired of thinking. That could come later. She wanted to come *now*. She sighed and relaxed into the bed, and he chuckled. "That's it." He flicked her with his fingertip and then suddenly pressed hard.

She screamed his name and arched off the bed again, twisting the sheets into wrinkled handfuls. Her orgasm blasted through her like a shock wave, the epicenter at his fingertip and radiating out to the far reaches of her body. She quivered and clutched at Jack, her only anchor in the most powerful climax of her life. He held her close and murmured to her in French again as she fought the pleasure and then finally surrendered to it. Surrendered to him. The shock wave became a soothing rocking and finally a ripple.

She opened her eyes and swallowed hard, her mouth dry. Jack stared down at her, his eyes wide. "What?" she asked.

He shook his head. "Only that that was the most beautiful thing I have ever seen. And that you would share it with me."

"Really?" She was sweaty and probably red as a beet, but he was looking at her as if she were the last truffle in France.

"Really."

She preened a bit. "I'm not done sharing with you, if you know what I mean." She reached down and cupped his cock, still stiff as a board after all that foreplay. Poor man, he was so patient. And so virile. She pulled him on top of her so he rested between her legs.

He groaned and thrust against her as she squeezed her thighs around his erection. "Oh, Lily."

"You like that?"

"I like everything you do to me." He nudged her legs wide open. "But I *love* being inside you." He plunged forward and sank deep into her.

His thick cock filled her sensitized center and she let out a short scream. He stopped for a brief second, but she smiled at him and he started to move inside her.

And like that, Lily was back in the realm of mindless lust, where her only thought was how soon she could come again. His flesh slapped into hers and pulled out, making her whimper until he filled her again. She hooked her legs around his waist to keep him locked inside but he couldn't keep still, his body in control and driving toward his own orgasm.

His body rubbed hers and she responded, tightening around him. His chest hair caught on her nipples, rasping their swollen peaks. He bent down and licked the top curve of her breast and then sucked hard on her nipple, sending exquisite jolts down to her clit.

She dug her fingers into his shoulders and moaned, "Jacky."

"That's it, Lily. Show me how much you want me," he commanded. He moved to her other nipple, leaving the first glistening and pink like a ripe berry.

Before she could stop herself, she nipped at his shoulder.

Jack grinned and lifted his head. "The little cat has claws and teeth. Maybe I can make you purr."

After that, Lily didn't purr as much as moan, pant and scream as he slammed into her, moving them across the bed until she was against the headboard. He hooked his hands under her shoulders and pulled her down under him, their sweaty skin clinging and releasing as his cock slapped wetly in and out of her pussy.

He stopped for a second and reached between their bodies to unerringly find her clit. A couple strokes and she clutched wildly as she spasmed around him. He thrust long enough to make sure she'd hit the highest peak and then let go of himself.

He tossed back his head, his eyes dark and blind to anything but the powerful spasms of his climax. His lips drew into a snarl as he roared his release like a lion who had claimed his mate.

It was the first time she'd been able to see his face at his peak and she was entranced. His easygoing, suave exterior was entirely gone, his primitive sexuality on display for only her to see. She held on tight to him as he gasped and collapsed. She welcomed his heavy weight pressing her into the bedding and inhaled the scent of their lovemaking rising from their skin.

"Ah, *ma belle* Lily." He was still breathing hard. "How can it be like this?"

She shook her head, enjoying how his chest rasped along her cheek, his heart thumping sturdily inside his ribs. "I don't know, but I'm not looking a gift horse in the mouth."

He laughed and rolled them to their sides. "I hope that I am not the gift horse, *non?*"

"No, you're the *stallion*." She wiggled her eyebrows lasciviously, making him laugh even harder. "How do you say that in French?"

"Oh, no, no." He shook his head. "I'll teach you any other French words you want, but not that."

"Okay, I'll ask the next Frenchwoman I meet. And if she asks why I want to know, I'll look at you and smile."

He groaned. "Ah, my reputation will never recover if you do that. *Stallion* is *étalon.*"

"Ay-tal-ohn," she mimicked. "My stallion."

"Ah, *mon dieu,* Lily." He laughed. "I never know what to expect from you."

"Is that a bad thing?"

"Not at all." Jack kissed her mouth and extricated himself from the rumpled bedding. "I'll be right back." He pulled on his briefs and disappeared downstairs, quickly returning with a pair of champagne flutes and a bottle of champagne. "I was going to do this first. Show you the house, offer you champagne, feed you and then…" He gave a shrug and laughed, setting down the glasses to open the bottle.

"Then this?" She pointed at her naked body. Somehow she wasn't shy around him.

"Only if you wanted." He poured the pale bubbly into the tall narrow glasses, designed especially so the bubbles would not immediately evaporate and flatten the wine.

"I did want."

"Good. So did I." He offered her a full champagne flute. "To this. To us."

They delicately touched the rims of what had to be fine crystal and Lily sipped, her eyes widening in shock. "No. This isn't—"

He gave her a sidelong glance. "Isn't what?"

"Did you open a bottle of Bollinger Blanc?"

"You have an excellent palate. That's exactly what it is. 1995, to be exact."

She sat bolt upright. "Jack! We can't accept their hospitality and then drink all the expensive wine. How tacky is that?"

"Not tacky at all. I bought it myself the last time I visited and we didn't get around to drinking it, that's all."

"Oh." She relaxed a bit. "But you really should replace it before we go, don't you think?"

"Of course. There is an excellent wine store in a nearby town. I'll order another bottle."

"Okay, but you have to let me help pay for it. You're not the only one drinking it, you know." She took another sip. It was the best champagne she'd ever tasted, and this time she had a whole glass of it, not just a stolen sip from an untouched party glass.

A whole glass…she dribbled some down her belly so it pooled in her navel. "Have a drink, Jack. Nice and wet, the way you like it."

His nostrils flared and he dipped his tongue in her belly button. "I like it all. I like you, nice and wet." He inhaled greedily. "I can smell myself on you, smell your arousal."

He drew lazy circles on her belly with his tongue and then stopped suddenly.

She nudged him to get him going again but he sat back on his haunches and gestured at her glass. "Have some more champagne."

"You don't have to get me drunk to have your wicked way with me. I'm perfectly willing." But she wasn't willing to let her champagne go flat, so she drank more.

"Bah," he puffed in disgust. "Real men do not need to get women drunk to make love. That is why we only went to sleep first our first night in Provence—you were tired and had much wine in addition. I would not take advantage of that."

"Good thing I sobered up in my sleep." She deliberately stretched and yawned, making sure her breasts pointed up invitingly.

He took a large mouthful of champagne and before she realized what he was doing, fastened his mouth on her nipple. She shrieked at first from the cold and then the bubbles popping against her tender skin. A chuckle rumbled through him, but he sucked at her with the sparkling wine.

He finally let go and swallowed. "Ah, what could be better?"

"Doing the same to my other nipple?" she suggested.

"Excellent." He complied with her request until both peaks were tingling. He refilled her glass and she spilled champagne onto his belly and licked it off. He was rock-hard again and inches from her lips, his head ripe and purple like a juicy sweet plum. And she knew just how to eat it.

She sat up and gave him a wicked smile before filling her mouth with champagne. His eyes widened. "Oh, no, Lily."

She smirked and closed her mouth around his plump flesh and it was his turn to arch off the bed in a howl of pure sensation. The bubbles buzzed him as she sucked on him. Champagne dribbled down his shaft as she took him deeper between her lips. He fisted his fingers through her hair, tiny pinpricks of pleasure and pain tingling her scalp.

"Enough," he growled, lifting her head so she released him.

"Don't you like that?" He'd sure seemed to enjoy it so far.

"Too much. I want to be inside you, want us to explode together." He pushed her onto her hands and knees and she heard a packet rip open. "Have you ever seen a stallion take a mare, Lily?"

She shook her head, quivering in anticipation as he moved behind her. He quickly found her clit, still throbbing and swollen from their previous loveplay. She tossed her hair back and he nudged her legs apart.

Jack covered her body with his, his chest on her back, his strong hands braced on the bed next to her smaller, more delicate ones. She expected to feel confined, intimidated, even frightened since he had the position of power and she couldn't see what he was doing. But there was no coercion in his actions, only security and shelter in his arms. "Take me like that, Jack."

"Yes..." he hissed and pushed inside her. Lily gave a little scream as he nipped at her neck. She bowed her head and saw her hard-tipped breasts swaying in time to his thrusts—the nipples he'd sucked on. Saw his thick erection moving in and out of her—the erection she'd sucked on. Their raw animal passion shocked her and aroused her to a fever pitch.

"You like it like this, don't you." It wasn't a question.

He could obviously feel how her body melted around him, wet and creamy.

"I want to feel you inside me."

"I am, *bébé,* I am." He shoved himself to the hilt to let her feel his power, his heft.

She shook her head, not daring to say what she wanted.

"What?" he soothed her. "Tell me what you want. I'll do anything you want."

She allowed her imagination to run wild for an instant, wanting the most impossible thing. "Inside me without the condom," she gasped. "Skin on skin. Feeling you shoot inside me when you come, hot and sticky."

"Oh, *merde.*" His reply was anguished and his whole body shook. "You'll make me come just by saying that. I want that too, but…" His cock pulsed inside her, as if readying to fire.

"Yeah, I know." Better to be safe than sorry. But it would be so intense for both of them.

"Lily, that would be my biggest fantasy." He moved inside her again, in and out. "When we were driving here today, I was thinking of how powerful that would be."

"Ohhh…" That was the cause of his arousal while driving. "No wonder you were so turned on."

He grunted, whether in passion or embarrassment, she didn't know. Or care, since he had seized her hips and was thrusting into her, hitting all the right spots. And then he reached around her and found her clit, and she screamed, coming really hard.

He followed her, his cock tensing and flexing inside her as he roared his release. He pulled out of her and eased them down to the bed.

Lily pried her eyes open and kissed his shoulder, the nearest body part she could reach without moving too much. Her eyes widened. "Geez, did I do that?"

"What?" He looked down at where she pointed to his chest. "A love bite." A smug smile spread over his face at the idea that she had bitten him in a fit of passion. Her own face flushed.

He laughed, a rich and hearty sound. "Why, Lily, you little savage." He sat up and turned his back to her. "Do I carry your claw marks, too?"

In fact, he did—eight red lines on his shoulders from where she clutched at him. He looked over his shoulder at her and lifted an eyebrow at her guilty expression. "Those, too, eh?"

"Oh, my God." She buried her face in her hands and rolled onto her stomach. How embarrassing to mangle the poor guy when all he was doing was helping her enjoy herself.

"Uh-uh." He rolled her back, his eyes warm and crinkling at the corners. "I knew the risks going in, but I will always be willing to sacrifice a few centimeters of epidermis for your pleasure."

She flicked her fingers against his upper arm. "Your pleasure, too, as if you didn't notice."

"I have rather delicate skin, you know." He scooped her into his arms, forestalling any of her attempts at retaliation. "All I ask is that you do not leave any permanent marks."

"Oh, Jack." She buried her face in his chest, his chuckle rumbling under her ear. She may have marked him physically, but he had marked her emotionally with his tenderness, his kindness and his care—and this was only after a few days. Once they parted, she would carry a mark more painful than any bruise or scratch.

11

LILY PADDED DOWNSTAIRS in her chocolate-brown shorts and white tank top after waking up alone in the pleasantly mussed big bed. After a couple peeks into a formal dining room, family room and study, she found him in the kitchen. "There you are, Jack." He sat at the big island in the middle of the room reading a newspaper.

"Have a good nap, Lily?" He set down the paper and swiveled to face her.

She nodded and yawned, her muscles pleasantly loose and relaxed from their romp upstairs and the nap that had followed it. She wrapped her arms around his waist and nuzzled his cheek. He was clean-shaven and smelled sunny, like lemons and green herbs. He must have showered while she was sleeping. "I've been asleep for a couple hours—you should have woken me up."

"You needed the rest." He kissed her neck and she half-heartedly pushed at him.

"Stop, Jack, I need to shower."

"Mmm, you smell great." He slipped his hand up her tank top, his long fingers unerringly finding her breast. "No bra, either."

Lily relaxed into his embrace and was beginning to

wonder if the granite countertop would feel terribly cold and hard on her back when her stomach growled. Not once, but three times.

Jack laughed and withdrew his hand, kissing her on the tip of her nose. "I am a poor host. We have been here for hours and the only thing we've had is some champagne."

She wiggled her eyebrows. "We've had a bit more than that."

He laughed and stood up. "Food for now. The pantry is usually well-stocked, and we can drive to town later for fresh bread, fruits and vegetables."

"And cheese, Jack. Ever since we had that wonderful late-night snack at the bed-and-breakfast, I've had a taste for goat cheese."

"Layered with fresh tomato and basil, drizzled with fine olive oil and cracked black pepper," Jack teased, making her mouth water.

"All right, you better get cooking." She shook her finger at him and he laughed.

"This is a beautiful kitchen, Jack." The big kitchen was bright and sunny, like everything in Provence. The walls were plastered in a creamy yellow, and the exposed ceiling beams were dark and weathered, as if they had been exposed to centuries of cooking smoke.

"I am glad you like it." He dug through the large fridge. "Hmm. Not a lot of fresh ingredients, but I can make some pasta. How does that sound?"

"Lovely." Lily hopped up onto the stool he'd vacated. The island's base was cream weathered oak cabinetry to match the rest of the kitchen.

"Good." Jack pulled out a large stockpot and filled it with water, setting it to boil. He went to the pantry and pulled out some cans and jars.

Lily was glad to have him cook but reminded herself to

take some pictures for her blog. She scanned the room—a big brick fireplace and a seating area with a leather couch made the area cozy. "But why the fireplace? It doesn't get terribly cold, does it?"

He nodded. "The fierce mistral wind can drop the temperature within minutes, and winter can be very damp and cold. We are thin-blooded here and not used to the low temperatures."

She had a flash of her and Jack sitting on the leather couch in front of a lit fire. He would hand her a glass of rich red wine (that always seemed more like a winter beverage) and they would toast each other before snuggling together.

She shook her head. Winter was months away. She was returning to New York, and Jack was returning to the next dangerous disaster area that came along—not exactly good for a relationship.

Lily hopped up and paced toward the wide picture windows overlooking the back garden. She opened the French doors and stepped onto the flagstone patio. Big terra-cotta pots of herbs dotted the edges. Basil, thyme and tarragon. The warm, dry weather here was perfect for growing herbs. There was even a row of rosemary bushes near a bench. "Parsley, sage, rosemary and thyme," she sang to herself.

"You have a lovely voice." Jack was leaning against the door frame, a small stainless-steel colander in one hand.

"No, I don't." She waved her hand dismissively. "The choir director at my school told me I'd never improve unless I had private lessons."

"And you didn't get to have lessons?" he guessed, coming onto the patio.

She shrugged. "It was only my mom and me growing

up, so it was hard for her to come up with the money for lessons."

"The two of you? And your mother never remarried?"

Lily had to smile. "She finally did after I was grown. At least Stan is good around the house." She burst out laughing.

"What?" Jack looked puzzled.

"Hmm." She stopped laughing and gave him a steady look. He'd been nothing but open and honest with her, and she'd been holding back from him. "Let's pick some herbs for the pasta."

He nodded, and they quickly selected some thyme, tarragon and a touch of savory. Lily rinsed the herbs off in the sink while Jack broke spaghetti noodles into the pasta pot and heated a sauté pan on the stove with a splash of olive oil and chopped garlic.

With his back to her, it was easier to tell her story. "I grew up in a house like that big manor house we passed on the way in."

He whipped around to look at her, a puzzled look on his face. Obviously she was not some rich girl out for a lark in Europe.

"My mother was the housekeeper," she clarified.

"Oh." He nodded. "Hence your taste for truffles and *foie gras.* You have a very sophisticated palate."

"Oui." She wrinkled her nose in amusement. "As the American phrase goes, I have champagne tastes with a beer budget."

"Another fascinating colloquialism. I am improving my English thanks to you every day."

She rolled her eyes in bemusement. He spoke better English than many native speakers.

"And you know I am more than happy to supply you champagne whenever you desire." The smoky look he shot her sent shivers down her spine. "But did the family you worked for treat you well?"

"Mrs. Wyndham isn't the warm and cuddly type, but she's always been fair with my mother and me," she allowed. "My father was killed in a car accident when I was a baby and my mother started working as an assistant to the housekeeper. When she retired, Mom took her job and we moved into the carriage house over the garage. It was bigger than the tiny Philly apartment we'd been living in and the countrylike atmosphere of the upscale Main Line suburb seemed like paradise."

Jack nodded as he sliced a narrow, pepperoni-like sausage into slices. "Rip up those herbs and tell me more."

Lily busied herself with pulling the fresh leaves from their stems, the spicy green scent a kind of aromatherapy. "You know, I never like talking about this."

He paused slicing and raised his head. "Why not? Are you ashamed of the work your mother did? That she was a servant?"

"Don't call her that!" Lily snapped without thinking.

He gazed at her steadily. "To serve is not a shameful thing. A widow with a small child would have had limited choices in careers—that is, if she wanted to keep you with her instead of giving you up to relatives or foster care."

Lily bit her lip.

"I am a servant, too," he continued. "I serve the poor and the needy instead of the rich. Does that make my work of even less value?"

"No." She struggled with a particularly tough stem but her hands were shaking with emotion. "That's different. That's charity—altruism for the less fortunate."

He set down the knife. "Charity begins at home. I know that American saying. But your mother did her work out of love for you, an even more powerful motivation."

Lily stared down at the green mess in her bowl. Jack dumped the cooked pasta into a colander in the sink and shut off the burner under the sauté pan.

He came around the island and gathered her into his arms. "I am sorry. This is a tender subject for you and you are hungry and tired."

She shook her head. "You're right. I guess I resent it sometimes. Being the poorest kid in a school full of rich ones wasn't the best situation."

"Oh, Lily." He started to say something and then stopped, kissing the top of her head.

She wrapped her arms around his waist and settled into his embrace. Had she ever really discussed her childhood with anyone but Sarah? She doubted it. "You make me think about things I don't usually think about."

"Then don't. Madame Finch would whack me with a ruler for treating you so poorly. We are here to relax and get to know each other, that's all."

How could she let him get to know her when she didn't know herself? For a writer, she was singularly not interested in self-reflection. Maybe that was why she wrote how-to and travel articles instead of weepy book-club memoirs. And really, what did she have to complain about? She sighed. Maybe it was time to look at her unusually overprivileged underprivileged childhood.

Jack pulled back so he could see her face. "Still want to eat?"

"Still want to feed me?" she parroted back.

"Of course." He planted a quick kiss on her lips and then rinsed the mass of pasta before tossing the sausage into the sauté pan. He pulled a jar of sun-dried tomatoes from the fridge and chopped them before adding them and the herbs to the pan. Once everything was heated through, he shook out the excess pasta water and dumped the noodles into the olive oil mix, stirring to coat them.

Lily found a couple plates and he served them heaping helpings with a generous grating of Parmesan cheese on top. While it cooled for a minute, he poured a ruby-red wine into what had to be Irish lead crystal—the real, handcut kind. *"Bon appétit."*

It was beautiful, had taken ten minutes and was straight from jars and boxes. A perfect recipe for her blog. "Wait a second." She sprinted upstairs and brought back her camera, taking several shots of the food and wine.

"All right, all right, enough with the photos," he finally said after a few minutes. "The pasta is getting cold and you need to eat."

She grumbled a bit but was secretly pleased at his concern for her well-being.

He raised his glass in a toast. "To Lily. I am so lucky we met."

"To Jack." She raised hers, as well. "For showing me the real France—and a lot of a certain real Frenchman."

He laughed and sipped his wine. "Eat, eat."

The food was exquisite, as good as any restaurant meal she'd had. "You're almost as good in the kitchen as my mother's new husband, Stan."

"Ah, you did mention he was skilled around the house— he can cook, as well?"

Lily couldn't help giggling. "I should hope so. He's the Wyndham family chef."

"Lovely!" Jack started to laugh. "The housekeeper finds happiness with the family chef."

"Their new house is spotless and they eat like kings. What more could you ask for?"

"Love." He said it so matter-of-factly that she knew he meant it. "If they have love, then nothing else matters."

"Nothing? Not money or age or different backgrounds?"

He was already shaking his head. "Nothing. Everything else can be dealt with, but love is the one thing that should never be compromised."

"They do love each other," Lily whispered. Sometimes it made her feel left out since it had been just Mom and her for so many years. But she was a woman now, and it was time to let her mother be a woman in her own right, as well. "Have you ever loved like that?" she blurted and then immediately blushed. If she were going to drink wine like a Frenchwoman, she needed to get better control of her tongue.

He stared steadily at her and she raised her glass to block the mortified expression on her face. He waited to answer her until she had set down her glass. She couldn't spend the entire meal hiding behind it, despite her cheeks that felt as red as the wine. "I thought I did once, but I was wrong. And you?"

Turnabout was fair play and she answered him as bluntly. "No, never. Not even close."

He nodded. "I know we are not in love, Lily, but I am glad we are lovers."

"Lovers." She tested the word on her lips, remembering the first time she had used it with the Frenchwoman on the train. Then, it had been awkward and embarrassing. But now that she and Jack truly were lovers, it was natural and freeing to say the word, at least with him. "Yes, I am glad, too."

Not that she would go around introducing him like that, as in, *Have you met my lover, Jack?* Really, a woman had to draw the line somewhere in maintaining some mystery.

"However long you want me—you want *us,* Lily," he promised solemnly.

That was what she wanted, too—but what if she wanted

him forever? The thought stunned her, and she used her jaw dropping as an excuse to shovel in a mouthful of pasta. *Lovers* did not equal *forever;* it was a live-in-the-moment kind of thing.

He watched her eat for a minute, satisfied that she was replenishing her body, and then settled down to his meal. They chatted as they ate, finding common interests in music, art and movies. They of course had different perspectives, but that made it more interesting to debate the fine points. He was witty and well-read, intelligent and amusing.

Lily paused for a second and looked at Jack and looked at their amazing meal. Their relationship was like the pasta—hot and fresh, but after a certain point would get cold and lumpy, not ever quite living up to its original flavor. But for now, oh, was it delicious.

THE NEXT DAY, Jack left Lily chatting with her cousin via webcam and headed out to meet Jean-Claude to talk about estate business. This was the first summer in many years that Jack had been in Provence for the lavender harvest, and Jean-Claude was eager to involve him. Probably so Jack wouldn't stay away so long again. Halfway up the hill to the field, his own phone rang.

He smiled at the display and answered it. *"Bonjour, chérie."*

"Oh, Jack, I'm so glad to talk to you. I was worried to death when George told me you were sick." It was Stevie, his little sister in all but DNA. Even though Princess Stefania was a beautiful grown-up lady, he couldn't help remembering her as the inconsolable twelve-year-old who had come to live with them after the death of her parents. George had been a sophomore at the university living off-campus with Jack and Frank, but had quickly hired a housekeeper to care for Stefania and make sure their flat wasn't condemned by the New York Board of Health.

"George tells me you are in Provence now. Good for you. I never liked Paris that much anyway."

He grinned. Translation: Stevie never liked his mother that much anyway, and had absolutely detested Nadine. "How else can I make sure your lavender will be ready for the *parfumerie?*"

"I know, and I'm absolutely thrilled you're doing this. I want to sell the perfume and give all the proceeds to my charity—you know, the obnoxiously named Princess Stefania of Vinciguerra Foundation for Women and Children?"

"Why is that obnoxious?"

"Because, dummy, my grandmother set it up when I was too young to know any better and named it after me, as if I wanted to blow my own horn. On the other hand, that self-servingly-named foundation is going to pay for several new schools in poor countries and is rescuing girls from sex slavery in Western Europe as we speak. But don't tell anyone about that last part, because I fund them under the table. Dangerous work, prying girls away from their pimps."

Jack's eyebrows shot up. "Am I to assume you've gone on these missions yourself?"

"Assume whatever you like," she said airily. "I will categorically deny we've ever had this conversation if necessary."

He shook his head. "Stevie, are you working for the CIA now?"

She laughed. "And if I did, would I tell you? Besides, I am a loyal subject of my brother and our principality."

Which wasn't much of an answer, but she had always been maddening in her own lovable way.

"Don't work too hard on the lavender harvest. Jean-Claude can handle it," she informed him.

"Stevie, I am not some ancient invalid. I have been quite active the past several days and have no ill effects." He smiled at the memory of several of his activities.

"What have you been up to?" Her tone was suspicious.

"What?" She caught him off guard. Maybe she did work for the CIA.

"What kind of activities?" she repeated and then paused. "You have a woman there with you, don't you?"

"I don't know what you mean," he replied with some dignity.

"Mmm-hmm. What's her name?"

"A gentleman never kisses and tells." And he wasn't going to talk about his sex life with Stevie.

"So you do have someone!" She sounded delighted. "Have Jean-Claude and Marthe-Louise met her yet?"

A reluctant laugh was dragged from him. "Stefania…"

"Uh-oh, you only call me that when you are trying to be stern and paternal. Tell me her name."

"Lily." It slipped out. But once he did, he couldn't stop grinning. He'd been hugging the secret of his new relationship to his chest like a teenager with a photo of a movie star, and Stefania was the first of his friends to learn about Lily. Next thing he knew, he'd be skipping through the lavender fields, sniffing a sprig and mooning over Lily. At least the field workers would get a hearty laugh.

"Really? I was just guessing, you know. Is she French?"

"American. But we met in Paris."

"An American in Paris." Stevie hummed a few bars of the Gershwin ballet. "Did you dance around the fountain with her?"

"I am no Gene Kelly." Jack smirked. Thanks to ten years of dance class, Stevie was extremely knowledgeable about ballet. Good thing she couldn't see him tap dancing around her inquisitive nature. "But we went to the Parc Buttes-Chaumont."

"How dreamy," she sighed. "You met, swept her off her feet and then whisked her off to your ancestral home in Provence. Jack, sweetie pie, you are becoming quite the romantic. You sound like those novels I love to read."

"Enough, enough." His cheeks were heating.

"Well, whoever Lily is, she can't be any worse than Nadine. Ugh."

"Stefania…" he said in warning.

She grinned. "Again with the stern authoritarian tone. But I also wanted to let you know Dieter and I have set our wedding date. We met with the bishop and chose a date next June because I want all the roses blooming for me. That's only eleven months away! And I want to give you enough time to make my perfume, right?"

"Of course. We will press the oil right after harvest and then you and the perfumer can create a blend and choose a bottle and packaging."

"Great, Jack." She blew kisses into the phone. "Take care of yourself," she reminded him. "No more parasitic infections for you. You and Frank are ushers at my wedding, so I want you to look good in your tux."

"It would be an honor."

"Maybe you can come see me in New York when you feel better?"

"Of course." They said their goodbyes and Jack hung up, staring thoughtfully across the purple valley of his farm.

Traveling to New York in a few weeks? Lily lived in New Jersey, a quick train ride from Manhattan. But did she want him to come visit her? He blew out a sigh of frustration. He hated uncertainty. As the old American saying went, failure to plan meant planning to fail.

What was his plan with Lily? He knew one thing, though—he didn't want her to leave. Was that a plan? To keep her with him indefinitely. Or forever?

12

LILY LOOKED UP from her computer screen and rolled her neck to loosen the kinks. She would much rather be smooching with Jack in the big bed upstairs, but she'd already neglected her blog for the past couple days to do just that.

Traffic was increasing. Sarah, although pretty much confined to her recliner at home, was doing a champion job of cross-posting her blog to various travel sites, sites aimed at young single women and foodie websites. Lily hadn't intended to be so food-oriented, but her photos of the Provence markets and descriptions of Madame Roussel's late-night hors d'oeuvres proved popular, according to her blog traffic stats.

Lily had mentioned "Pierre" a few times in her blog posts. Not the sex parts, obviously, because it wasn't that kind of a blog. Sarah was already anxious about Lily traveling with Jack. She didn't need to get all the lurid details. Lily might tell her at some later date, but only when Lily was safely back home.

At this point, Lily would take all the traffic she could get. She got up and walked around the desk. Jack had set her up in the guesthouse study, which was a far cry from her makeshift "office" at her breakfast bar at home.

A wall of books stood behind the desk, which was a rustic-looking wooden plank several inches thick varnished and fastened to four heavy square legs. It matched the exposed beams in the ceiling and was big enough to spread out several reference books on Provence—cookbooks with mouth-watering recipes, coffee-table photo books of breath-taking photography and of course an assortment of memoirs and travelogues describing falling-down farmhouses, weed-choked olive groves and robust peasant neighbors.

But all Lily had to do was look out the floor-to-ceiling picture windows to see Provence for herself. The study was tucked into the corner of the house where she could see the lavender fields and upright, skinny evergreens, and nary a weed or crumbling building in sight. Jack's friends certainly had pride in their property.

Pride and lots of money. She'd grown up around it and could smell it, like a new dollar bill fresh from the mint.

Lily's email program dinged and she found a new message. Ooh, from Margo, an editor at *Fashionista Magazine.* But why would she want to email her? She wasn't writing about clothes, and her own fashion style on this trip had consisted of either hiking outfits or being buck naked.

She clicked on the icon and read the screen, stunned. The editor was interested in her blog and wanted her to write an online column on traveling in France from the point of view of a hip, single woman. Lily rolled her eyes. She didn't know how hip she was, but, hey, she could fake it.

She read on. Oh. They wanted her to write about Frenchmen in general, "Pierre" in particular. She'd never shown Jack's face in any photos she'd posted, but perhaps the element of mystery had intrigued the editor, who had left her number with an invitation to call her for more details.

Ten minutes later after calling New York, Lily had agreed to posts every other day, which would be linked on the magazine site's home page. And Margo had hinted there would be more work for her, maybe even feature articles in the print version of the magazine. Lily didn't know exactly what her topics might be, since she wasn't going to travel around Europe dating more men just so she could write about them. Professional dating was not to her liking.

She and Margo had agreed on some boundaries for her blogs. The editor, of course, was interested in as much juicy detail as Lily would offer, but Jack had a vested interest in not becoming the latest internet heartthrob.

She'd have to double-check with him about being a semifictional character in her blog—names and details changed to protect the innocent, as they said on TV.

Jack came into the study. *"Bonjour, chérie."* He leaned over the desk and kissed her.

"Guess what, Jack?" She told him about her new writing job.

"I am not surprised at your success, Lily. Your sincere interest in my country comes through in your work."

She took a deep breath. "The editor wants me to write about you, as well."

"Me?" His eyebrows shot up. "But you have hardly mentioned me and you aren't even using my real name."

"She says American women are fascinated by Frenchmen and wants more detail about dating and romance in France. But I don't want to put any of our own personal situation online," she added hastily.

He rubbed his chin. "Dating and romance in France is

much the same as anywhere else, but I'm sure you and I can think of something that editor might like. But again, I have to ask you not to post any photos that show my face."

"I won't," she promised.

"What would you like to do this afternoon? Research French romance?"

Lily pressed her lips together and thought. The view out the window caught her eye again. "Get a tour of the manor house."

He blinked in surprise.

"That is, if your friends don't mind," she amended, not wanting to be a bad guest.

"Hmm." He rubbed his chin thoughtfully. "Marthe-Louise would be delighted to show us around."

"Great." Lily shut down her computer and grabbed her camera. "Let's go."

DELIGHTED WAS AN understatement—the plump woman in her fifties was ecstatic to see Jack. If she'd been any younger, Lily would have been jealous.

"Jacques, oh, *mon petit* Jacques!" She spotted them at the kitchen door and wiped her hands on her apron before dragging Jack inside.

"Marthe-Louise is the housekeeper here," he called, as the older woman plastered his cheeks in teary kisses.

"She certainly remembers you fondly."

He grinned ruefully and said something soothing to Marthe-Louise, patting her shoulder. "Okay, Marthe-Louise, this is Lily. Lily, this is Marthe-Louise."

"Lee-Lee!" Marthe-Louise released Jack and seized Lily, kissing her vigorously twice on each cheek. She unleashed a torrent of excited French. "Ah, *belle, belle, si belle!*"

"She says you are very beautiful."

Lily blushed and Marthe-Louise cooed and pinched her reddening cheek before asking Jack a question.

He nodded and replied at length. The housekeeper gave him an exasperated look but finally nodded her head.

"Merci." Jack blew the older woman a kiss and she giggled. "She will give us a tour of the house but needs to straighten up a bit first."

"Oh, okay." The house looked immaculate, but there was probably a pile of mail here and a newspaper there that would take away from the manorial splendor.

The housekeeper darted out and returned in a couple minutes.

The house was impressive, with a huge salon and dining area for hosting large soirées, several sitting rooms, a giant library filled with books that Lily itched to read and a glass-enclosed conservatory, or *orangerie,* where they grew potted orange and lemon trees for fresh fruit during the winter.

It was a massive building, but with few personal touches and no family portraits. Probably those were upstairs in the living quarters, which weren't part of the tour.

They returned to the kitchen, easily twice the size of the kitchen at the guesthouse. *"Ongree?"* Marthe-Louise asked.

"What?" Lily asked politely.

"You *ongree?*" she asked her.

"Oh, hungry." Her stomach growled and they all laughed. "Yes, I am hungry."

The housekeeper flew into action and quickly had a platter of crusty sliced bread with a variety of spreads in little ceramic pots.

Jack pointed to one pot and then the next. "Olive and dried figs for a sweet-and-salty mix, fresh tuna and olive, and chickpeas with cumin—a variation on hummus."

"And pasta," Marthe-Louise added. "Jack, he no tell *moi* he come. Bad, bad boy." She retaliated by smacking his arm. "I cook now."

Jack opened a cabinet and got out three wineglasses. He opened the under-counter wine refrigerator and pulled out a couple different bottles before settling on a white wine. He certainly was making himself at home in the manor house kitchen, and Lily glanced nervously at Marthe-Louise to make sure she didn't think it was presumptuous.

Jack set the full glass next to the housekeeper's elbow, and she thanked him, so it wasn't a problem for her. Lily relaxed a bit, especially when he lifted his glass in a toast. "*A votre santé.* To your health."

"And to yours." He had lost the gaunt, pale look in his cheeks and this giant lunch would help fill out the rest of him. "*Bon appétit.*" He and Marthe-Louise smiled approvingly at her French.

Lily didn't know if *gorged* was quite the right word to describe what she and Jack did to the little slices of breads and savory toppings, but once she took artsy, foodie photos of the Provence-made yellow ceramic dish with its black fig spread and the red ceramic dish with the creamy tan chickpea spread, *gorged* came close. Good thing tuna spread wiped off her phone, which she used to make notes for her next blog.

Marthe-Louise was pouring a green sauce into her top-of-the-line food processor to blend with several cloves of garlic and a couple egg yolks while a pasta pot bubbled on the stove. She stopped to shake a spoon at Jack and scold him.

"Okay, okay." He laughed. "We should save some room for her spaghetti."

Lily obediently put down her last crust of bread. She really needed to get some physical exercise in or else she would need to buy a second seat for her plane ride back to New York. Her plane ride scheduled four days from now. Well.

Marthe-Louise drained the spaghetti and poured in the rich green sauce, letting it sit.

Lily elbowed Jack. "Those are raw egg yolks. Haven't you had enough digestive problems?"

He whispered back, "Those are from her very own chickens and the heat of the pasta cooks them. No bad eggs allowed. Except for me, of course."

She giggled. Jack was about as far from a bad egg as you could find in a man. "You're a good egg." She rested her hand on his knee and aimed a kiss for his cheek.

He turned his head and her kiss landed on his mouth. He deepened the kiss and Lily opened her lips under him. He tasted spicy and warm, and she promptly forgot they weren't alone until he broke the kiss and smiled at her.

"Ah, l'amour, c'est grand!" Marthe-Louise was smiling too, and Lily blushed at the housekeeper's mention of love. The older woman gave Jack a doting glance as she dished green pasta. "Eat, eat. Then go sleep."

"How about it? Do you feel like an afternoon nap?" Jack murmured.

"Do we have to sleep?" she replied, and he laughed again, a hearty, baritone sound.

"Not unless you want to." He twirled a forkful of noodles and popped it into her mouth.

"Oh, yum." The garlic and basil mixed with the creamy egg yolks slid perfectly over the firm spaghetti.

Jack took a bite and hummed in pleasure, calling compliments to Marthe-Louise, who modestly waved a spoon at him.

They nibbled away at the pasta until Lily really did feel tired. "Jack, about that nap…"

He pushed away his bowl as well and glanced at the old ceramic clock on the countertop. "It is siesta time, and I have had enough carbohydrates to knock me unconscious."

"Let's be unconscious together." Lily hopped off the stool and wavered slightly. Jack steadied her.

"*Au revoir,* Marthe-Louise." He kissed her three times and pinched her cheek. She put one arm around him and scolded him affectionately, waggling her finger in his face. He protested tolerantly, gesturing nearly as much as she did. "She says to stop by anytime and she will cook us anything we want. She won't be happy until I am round and portly like her husband, Jean-Claude. He has never been sick a day in his life thanks to her cooking."

The housekeeper nodded emphatically, pushing a platter of pastries and a second bottle of wine into their hands.

"An afternoon snack?" Lily asked.

"For later. I may burst at any minute." He blew Marthe-Louise a kiss, leading Lily out of the kitchen to the gravel driveway leading to their guesthouse.

"She certainly takes good care of you. She knew you were sick?"

"Yes, but really, she's usually like that anyway. Eat, eat, eat. It's a good thing the men around here have physical jobs to burn off all the good cooking. And me, who practically has a doctor's prescription to do nothing but gain weight? A dream come true."

He was, but not necessarily in the culinary arena. Marthe-Louise obviously loved Jack like a son. She'd seen her own mother make sure Mrs. Wyndham was well-fed and living in clean surroundings, but her mother had never evinced this degree of maternal affection toward a guest of the family—she'd saved all that for Lily. She blurted, "I should call my mother."

"Of course," he said easily. "Feel free to use the phone

at the guesthouse." He shifted the wine bottle under his opposite arm and offered her his elbow. The gravel crunched under their feet as they strolled uphill. The air was hot and still, the buzz of the cicadas crescendoing with the rising afternoon temperature.

"I have an international plan on my cellphone." It would be almost cheaper to fly home to talk with her mother in person if they spent much time on the phone.

"Unnecessary," he said promptly. "Marthe-Louise would have my head if I let you do that."

"Hmmph." She'd leave some money on the counter to pay for her bill.

Jack showed her how to dial internationally and kissed her forehead. She stared dreamily after him and then snapped to attention as her mother's voice came on the line.

"Hello?"

"Mother? It's Lily."

"Lily. Are you well?" Her mother sounded pleased to hear from her.

"Yes, I'm fine. How are you?" For someone who attempted to make a living with her words, she was certainly falling short.

"Very good. I read your blog about how you're in Provence now."

Lily winced. She should have called her mother about her change in plans, but she'd sent her an email and was too used to doing things on her own. "Yes, and it's beautiful here. I'm in the middle of the lavender harvest and got some great photos that I'll post later as soon as I get the blog post written."

"Sarah told me how to subscribe to your blog, so I've been reading all your posts. You met a man named Pierre in Paris?"

"Yes, well, that's not his real name. I don't mind the publicity, but he works for a government agency and doesn't want his name splashed around the internet."

"Oh, my." Mother sounded amused. "Is he a French secret agent?"

Lily laughed. "No, he does relief work overseas and they go into dangerous regions sometimes. Publicity would put them at risk."

"Well, as long as you know his real name. I assume he is with you in Provence?"

Lily squirmed. Her mother didn't need to know all the details of her traveling—and sleeping—arrangements, so she settled for a bare-bones outline. "He comes from here, so we're staying at a guesthouse that belongs to his friends. The housekeeper fixed us several kinds of spreads and crackers and then we had this Provençal version of pesto sauce and spaghetti."

"Be sure to write down the recipes," Mother reminded her. "Although the ingredients somehow taste different when they are grown somewhere else. Much like the homemade *foie gras*—I enjoyed your post about that."

"Holy cow, was that good."

"I think you mean 'holy goose,'" her mother teased.

Lily was taken aback for a second but then joined in the laughter. Mother had never laughed or shown much of a sense of humor in years past. Stan the Chef (Stan her Stepdad, she reminded herself) was a jolly guy, and maybe he was helping her mother lighten up. "And how is Stan?" she asked.

"Fine, thank you for asking." Her mother sounded pleased at her interest. "He's at the market right now shopping for a dinner party tonight. Mrs. Wyndham is hosting one of the U.S. senators—he's up for reelection next year and is working on his fundraising."

Lily made a terrible grimace. "Good grief, Mother, those dinners are even more deadly than her usual parties."

"That's right, dear, you never did like that part of the job."

"But, Mother, how can you stand doing that stuff after all these years?" Lily burst out. "Don't you want to do something else before—?" she broke off her sentence.

"Before I get too old and feeble to work?" her mother replied. Fortunately she seemed more amused than offended. "Unfortunately I'm not even fifty yet, so retirement is a bit away."

Lily winced. She always forgot how young her mother was, only twenty when Lily was born.

"Besides, I'm not like you, Lily. I don't get bored easily and I enjoy routines and organization. For me, life is better when I know what's happening next."

"Gee, you sound like Jack. He's very organized and a real homebody, too."

"So your mystery Frenchman is named Jack?"

"Jacques, actually."

"I assume he's treating you well?" Mother's voice took on a steely tone she reserved for rich, drunken letches and lazy housemaids.

"Very well, Mother. I wouldn't be here otherwise."

"Good." Her tone softened. "I wish I had seen things differently when you were younger. I didn't understand your situation at school."

"Well, rich guys are pigs."

"Lily!" her mother scolded her. "Those particular young men were pigs, but don't be a reverse snob."

She shifted on the desk chair, remembering how she had accused Jack of snobbery, and that had proven so untrue as to be laughable. "Sorry." But he was just a regular guy anyway.

Mother was never one to harp on an admonishment. "When do you come back, dear?"

"My ticket is up in four days." Unless she extended her stay. Maybe there would be a general strike and they'd close the airports. That grim thought cheered her up.

"Please call when you get back. And come see us here in Philly. We've finished remodeling the carriage house kitchen and it's Stan's pride and joy."

"He cooks at home?" Why would he want to, after a long day in the kitchen at the main house?

Mother giggled like a teenager. Lily's jaw fell open—she'd never heard that sound before. "Sure, he does. He takes good care of me." That simple statement, filled with pride and love, made Lily's heart flip and her eyes tear.

"He'd better," she blustered, sniffing discreetly. "Or else I'll hide his favorite knives and sharpening stone." She'd grown up in a kitchen and knew how to punish a chef.

"Oh, my, how fierce." Her mother laughed again but cleared her throat. "And Lily, be careful with this man. I would hate to see you hurt."

"Mother, he's very nice."

"A nice man can break your heart as easily as a bad man. Sometimes worse, because you're not expecting it." Her tone had the ring of past experience.

Lily hesitated, but didn't know how to reply. "I understand," she finally said.

"I hope you won't have to," she said simply. "But keep up the good work and get those recipes for Stan and me," she emphasized with a chuckle.

Lily agreed and blew a kiss into her phone before hanging up.

Mother had found happiness after heartbreak and many long, hard years alone. Lily knew she wasn't ready to settle down herself, but couldn't help wondering what the future would bring.

Hopefully not heartbreak, but like Mother had said, it was unexpected. Lily just hoped Jack wouldn't be the one to bring it.

13

LILY SAT CROSS-LEGGED on the stone patio behind the guest-house kitchen, her camera aimed at an industrious bee buzzing around a purple sage plant. Not being a fan of bee stings, she moved slowly to frame her shots. One set had the golden-and-black insect in front of a solid wall of purple blooms, and for the second set, she lay down on her back and aimed upward. That angle showed the bee more in profile against the blue, blue sky.

She took a few pictures of the sky to capture the color. No wonder painting legends like Cézanne and Van Gogh, Picasso and Matisse had immortalized Provence in their art. She only wished she had the talent to do the same.

Ah, well. Her talent was with words, and maybe her photos would illustrate the land in some small way.

A shadow fell over her and, still looking through the viewfinder, she rotated to see Jack looking down at her. She fired off a couple shots of him silhouetted against the sky.

He looked startled. "That's an odd angle for a photo. Wouldn't you like my regal profile instead?" He turned his head to the right and put his finger under his chin, staring haughtily into the distance.

"I'm aiming for the artsy look. Don't worry, I won't put that one on my blog. But you do have that snooty expression just right."

He chuckled and extended a hand to her, the bee buzzing around him for a second until it decided to find greener pastures.

"You must not be scared of bees," she told him, standing and shutting down her camera.

He grinned. "Working on a flower farm knocks that out of you pretty fast. I don't *bug* them and they don't *bug* me."

She groaned at his pun.

"Bee-sides," he continued, "you have probably never had lavender honey. It is a local delicacy and Marthe-Louise has a wonderful recipe of duck glazed with lavender honey."

"Oh, yum. Do you think she would give me the recipe?"

He shrugged. "Sure, but she'll cook it for us if we ask."

"We could bring her the ingredients."

Jack rubbed his chin. "Let me talk with her and see what she would prefer. I know she has a little understanding with the butcher and likes to pick out her own fowl."

"The sign of a true artist," she told him. "Stan would never let anyone else pick the giant beef roasts that Mrs. Wyndham likes to serve at her dinner parties."

"Fortunately for us today, we will benefit from Marthe-Louise's culinary generosity. You can't come to Provence in the summer and not have a picnic. She fixed us a basket full of food and we're going up into the hills for the afternoon."

"Great." Lily tightened the laces on her sturdy hiking boots and socks. Bees and bare feet were a bad combination. "We've been staying close to home for the past several days."

"I haven't heard any complaints." He nuzzled her neck. "On the other hand, we could eat here. Later." She shivered as he nibbled her ear. "Much later."

"Oh, no, you don't." She pushed him away, though gently.

"Rejected." He pressed a hand to his heart.

"Hardly." Jack laughed and Lily realized her unintended pun. "Oh, you." She started to blush and his grin widened.

"Yes, me indeed. But alas, it is picnic time." He locked the back door of the guesthouse and they went around to the driveway. The picnic basket was already waiting in the car's backseat, and they drove up a dusty road deeper in the hills.

They stopped at a field full of workers. "Would you like to see how they harvest the lavender?"

"Absolutely."

A couple dozen harvesters, mostly young men and a few women, straightened as they approached. An older man started to chastise them for pausing but caught sight of Jack. He shouted a greeting. "Eh, M'sieu le...Jacques!"

He rapidly picked his way across the lavender field like a plump but nimble ballerina, not trampling or bruising a single plant. He wore a button-down shirt that had seen better days, a vest with several pockets, work boots and a round, flat-topped hat that she had seen on several of the older men. His face was round as well, bisected by a luxurious black mustache. "Jacques, *mon brave.*" He slapped Jack on the back. "And who is this?" he asked in heavily accented English.

"Lily, this is Monsieur Jean-Claude Chailan, husband of Marthe-Louise. Jean-Claude, this is Mademoiselle Lily Adams from America."

"Pleased to meet you." Lily extended her hand.

"Ah, Mademoiselle Lily, I am sorry we have not met

before. I have been supervising the farm workers and Jacques has been keeping you all to himself." Jean-Claude swept off his hat and actually bowed to her. He replaced his hat and clasped both of her hands, gazing at her with such a fond expression that she was momentarily taken aback. She saw the cheek-kiss routine coming, though and was prepared for it, although the third and fourth kisses were a surprise. Jack had told her that a fourth kiss was basically reserved for special occasions.

Jean-Claude drew back, still holding her hands in his work-hardened ones. "Ah, Mademoiselle, my good wife said you were beautiful, and I can see she was not exaggerating."

Lily reddened and Jean-Claude shook his head. "Ah, the touch of the rose on your cheeks. Jacques, you old dog, what did you ever do to deserve such a pretty girl?"

"Nothing, *mon ami,* nothing."

"Too true." The older man barked out a loud laugh. "Eh, but I should not tell all of your secrets today, no?"

"No," Jack said firmly.

"Oh, you've known each other a long time, then?" Lily asked.

"A lifetime, *chérie,*" Jack answered. "Jean-Claude came to Provence with the Roman legions and liked it so much he stayed."

Jean-Claude gave him a narrow stare. "Are you calling me an old man?"

"Just joking," Jack said hastily. "You are a man of experience, seasoned like an expensive red wine."

"That is better, you young punk." Jean-Claude let go of Lily's hands and slapped Jack on the back again. He bent and broke off a lavender sprig. "*Voilà,* Mademoiselle. This is the best lavender in France." He offered it to her.

Lily inhaled deeply. The perfume spiraled up into her nose, making her almost dizzy with the ripe scent.

Jack steadied her. She smiled at the men. "Powerful. But it doesn't smell like what I'm used to."

"You are used to the scent of the lavandin plant, a sterile hybrid that has more of a woodsy, camphor smell," Jack told her.

"Good for soap and clothes washing, but perfume—bah!" Jean-Claude waved his hands dismissively. "No good unless you want to smell like laundry." He puffed out his chest. "In fact, we are providing the lavender oil for an upcoming royal wedding. The bride is creating a perfume to be sold for her children's charity."

"Fascinating." Lily turned to Jack. "Did you know about this?"

"Many of the details are hush-hush, right, Jean-Claude?"

The older man put a finger to his mustache in a shushing gesture. "But of course."

Lily was disappointed not to have a big scoop like this but she wasn't some tabloid journalist to snoop around. "Tell me all the details as soon as you can."

Jean-Claude spread his hands wide. "I promise, you will be the first to know." His stomach growled loudly. "Lunch!" he called to the crew, who cheered and straightened. "I would invite you to eat with us, but Marthe-Louise told me you are going on a picnic."

"I thought we'd go to the northeast field. It has a great view and some shade."

"Ah, *oui,* that field will be ready for harvest next week. But not yet—there will be no one around." Jean-Claude didn't quite wink or waggle his eyebrows, but Lily got the gist of it.

"*Merci,* Jean-Claude. We'll see you later." Jack put his

arm around Lily's shoulders and they strolled back to the car.

The northeast field was as beautiful as the lower field, overlooking the valley. A large oak tree stood nearby, and Jack spread out their picnic blanket underneath it.

"What did Marthe-Louise pack for lunch?" Lily asked eagerly.

He opened the big cooler and handed her a plate from the smaller bag of supplies. "Cold roasted chicken, ham on baguettes, a wheel of goat cheese, crackers, fruit and her special potato—green bean salad with an oil-and-vinegar dressing."

Lily's mouth watered as he served her a heaping plateful. "Any dessert?"

"But of course." He grinned at her, lifting a container. "Cherry tarts, made fresh from our own trees."

She moaned in anticipation, and he laughed. "I've heard you make that sound before."

She swatted at him with her fork. "I enjoy the basics of life."

"And that is why you fit in so well here." He gestured to the beautiful farmland and perfect weather. "The basics of life are the best things in life." He pulled out a bottle of white wine and deftly decanted it into two goblets. Marthe-Louise had thought of everything.

Lily raised hers. "A toast to the most beautiful day in the most beautiful place on earth."

"To the most beautiful woman on earth." He raised his in return.

"Where?" Lily looked around, half in jest, but subsided when he gave her a stern look. "Well, um, thank you."

"To the most beautiful woman on earth," he repeated, and they touched rims.

"A votre santé." She remembered the traditional French toast to his health.

Jack smiled approvingly. "Very good." They drank some wine and did their best to do justice to Marthe-Louise's picnic.

Between the wine, the sun and the hypnotic buzzing of the cicadas, Lily's eyes started to droop by the end of the meal.

"Come lie down, *chérie,* we will have dessert later." He cleared the remnants of their meal and beckoned to her.

"Only for a little," she insisted. He nodded and she rested her head on his shoulder, closing her eyes.

It seemed like only a few minutes later, but the angle of the sun had dropped when she opened her eyes to find Jack watching her, an indescribable expression of tenderness on his face.

Without saying a word, she reached for him. Their clothes quickly disappeared and he was inside her, their gazes still locked. She didn't close her eyes until her senses were overwhelmed with the touch of his body, the scent of the lavender, the heat of the day and the blue of the sky.

They came simultaneously, and stayed in each other's arms for another eternity. Lily wondered at the perfection of it all, knowing she was at least half in love with Jack, if not totally. And remembering the expression on his face as she'd awoken, she thought he might feel the same way.

LILY SHUT DOWN her laptop after webchatting with Sarah. Her cousin was predictably over the moon with her pregnancy, which was continuing well, but not so engrossed that she forgot to warn Lily about the dangers of strange men, particularly strange Frenchmen.

Sarah had lowered her voice, presumably not to have her husband, Carl, overhear, and said, "Lily, believe me,

I spent a whole year and several summers there. I know how sexy and charming they can be. There was this one chef in Lyon who could do the most amazing things with chocolate…" Her voice trailed off and her eyes got dreamy for a second as Lily watched in amusement. "But that's not the point."

"The point is that I am being careful and having as much fun with Jack as you did with your pastry chef."

"That much, huh?" Sarah had sighed in nostalgia. "Oh, well, all of that is off my plate, so to speak, until I hear the all-clear from the doc. I'll get the details from you at some point, but not now."

Lily smiled as she remembered all the so-called details of last night. She stretched and stood up from the desk. Jack was up in the lavender fields with Marthe-Louise's husband Jean-Claude. Lily worried about him overexerting himself, but Jean-Claude seemed to look after Jack like a kindly old uncle.

The morning sun and sky were too nice to waste indoors. She ran upstairs and pulled on her swimsuit, a lime-green string bikini. Only old ladies wore one-piece suits in France. Even then, they rolled down the top and went topless like everyone else at the beach.

No issues like that at their private pool, however. Thanks to *Oncle* Pierre's privacy issues, a high limestone wall surrounded the pool area.

She went downstairs with a towel and grabbed a bottle of sparking water and a bowl of plump red grapes.

She carried her snack outside and decided to get some color, lying down on the large chaise lounge. With her round-framed sunglasses and pricey French water, she felt positively decadent. All she needed was a pool boy.

She closed her eyes and tipped her face up to the

sun. She drifted in and out of sleep, enjoying the lavender-and-rosemary scented breeze.

"A good idea on such a hot afternoon."

Ah, there was the pool boy. She opened her eyes to see Jack wearing a tiny competitive-swimmer type suit.

"Ack, what is that?" She still wasn't used to European-style men's swimsuits.

"Oh, is this the clothing-optional pool? I should have realized." He hooked his thumbs in the waistband and calmly pulled them off, kicking them away.

"Jack!" Sure, she'd been naked with him, and in daylight, too, but that time in the lavender field had seemed like a dream.

"Come on, sunbathe topless. You're in France, you know."

"Oh, fine." She rolled onto her stomach, untying the bottom string so her back was bare. She rested her face on her arms, ignoring his laughter. "If you want to get sunburned on your...well, that's up to you."

He laughed even harder and sat next to her. "Maybe you could put some sun lotion on my...well..."

Lily rolled onto her side. "Oh, yeah? And why should I do that?"

"I'd do the same for you." He wiggled his eyebrows suggestively.

She looked down and saw her top had shifted to the side, baring her breasts. "Hmmph." She unknotted the tie at her neck and tossed the two triangles aside.

"Ah, that's better," he said in appreciation. "We'll make a Frenchwoman out of you yet."

She sniffed. "Somehow I can't imagine your Provence ladies wanting to sunbathe topless." The image of Marthe-Louise getting a lineless tan was a bit much to imagine.

"You'd be surprised." His deadpan expression amused her. Who knew what these staid matrons got up to?

Jack was not tan all over, either. Working shirtless with Jean-Claude had browned up his torso, but he had a definite tan line at his waistband. Somehow, though, she didn't think he'd come out to even up his color, considering how hard and aroused he was growing under her gaze. "Good thing you took off your suit. You might have hurt yourself trying to fit all that inside."

He crawled up the lounge and positioned himself between her thighs. "But I like fitting myself inside...you, that is." The tip of his erection prodded the thin green fabric of her bikini bottom.

He was so big and hard and hot on top of her, a summer god come to life and wanting to have his way with her. Her nipples tightened in anticipation.

"Chilly?" He lifted an amused eyebrow. It was at least eighty-five degrees outside. She pursed her lips and he laughed. "Mmm, let me warm you up." He lowered his mouth to one tight pink peak and drew it into his mouth.

Lily was burning up. Jack licked her gently, first back and forth, then with round swirling strokes around her whole areola. Then a hard suck and a little nip. She gasped in a mix of shock and pleasure, and then he soothed her with his tongue. He lifted his head to admire his work. Her nipple was like a berry, firm and reddish pink, glossy and ripe.

"Oh, Lily, I could suck on your pretty tits for hours." He blew a cool stream of air over her wet flesh and she bit back a scream. He shook his head disapprovingly. "Don't you want to scream for me?"

"Well..."

"Don't be so shy. No one is around."

"Are you sure?" she whispered.

He laughed. "Jean-Claude is a stern taskmaster. Everyone is in the upper fields to harvest the prime lavender crop. Where we were the other day."

"Why aren't you?"

"There are benefits to being the…guest. Enough of that business. You are my business now." He moved to her other nipple and gave it his full attention.

The first wasn't neglected, though. His long, clever fingers caught it and gave it several gentle tugs. The double attention was more intense than anything, making her hips start to writhe under his.

He angled his erection so she rubbed up and down his length. He moaned against her breast and then his fingers were undoing the side ties of her bikini.

The fabric easily fell away and he was pressing on her, almost into her. He was so hard, and she was so wet. She shifted slightly so his tip entered her.

His eyes flew open. "Lily, the protection." They were both gasping at the new, erotic sensation. "Let me go get a condom."

"Why not like this? I'm on the Pill and healthy. Aren't you?"

"Not on the Pill." He gave a choked laugh. "But healthy. I've been tested for every infectious disease known to man."

Jack was wavering, she could tell. But it was his decision.

He surrendered with a groan and slid all the way into her to his hilt. She automatically locked her legs around him and they both stared at each other.

"I've never done this before," she confessed.

"Me, neither." He closed his eyes and shuddered. "Oh, Lily, it's beyond words."

"Tell me," she coaxed.

"You're burning me up, my sweet. Your heat, your creamy juices on my skin." He started moving inside her. "You make me crazy for you."

She tipped her head back. Every part of him touched her, unblunted by any barrier. His juices mixed with hers, making his thrusts even more slippery and delicious. Her plump, swollen nipples caught in his russet chest hair and she cooed in pleasure at the rough texture.

"Ah, you like, eh?" He picked up his pace, slamming inside her as she moaned with every jolt. "You're such a bad girl, Lily. I shouldn't do this, but I can't help myself. Sexy girl. Naughty girl."

Lily had never thought of herself as bad, sexy or naughty, but it sounded fun.

Suddenly, he raised his head. "Uh-oh."

"What?" She looked around but Jack kept thrusting into her.

"I think someone's there."

"What? Who?" She stopped moving but her body was drawing her on, not letting her matching thrusts stop.

His brown eyes were mischievous. "Someone who might hear how much you like this."

She moaned, sinking into the lounge, letting his fantasy take her away.

"Someone who wonders how wild you get with a bare cock inside you." He moved his hand between their bodies. "How wild you get with a finger on your clit." He touched her and she screamed. "Like that."

"Jacky…" she moaned.

"I love it when you call me that. Only you, *mon coeur* Lily."

She swallowed hard in a wave of sudden emotion. He called her "his heart." She threw her arms around him and kissed his neck, his chest, wherever she could reach.

He responded by renewing his touches and caresses, worshiping her body with his as they moved together as one.

She dug her fingers into his back and tightened around him. He caught her earlobe between his teeth and flicked it with his tongue. She arched into him and broke apart, her climax pitching her up fast and strong. "Oh, Jacky, Jacky…"

He pushed with one last strong thrust and groaned, his head tossed back with all the cords in his neck pulling taut.

He flooded into her and she climaxed again, even harder. He called her name over and over again and she loved how his French accent got thicker during passion. She clung to him, almost desperately as they gasped for air.

He slumped on top of her, resting his head next to hers against the lounge cushion. She kissed his cheek and he turned his face to softly kiss her lips.

"You are wonderful, Lily. So much fire when we make love."

Love.

A ray of sun lit up his hair as she twisted her fingers around a strand of burnished copper. He was heat and fire and tenderness and…love?

He lifted his head and smiled sweetly at her. "What is it?"

"Nothing." She hadn't meant for him to notice. But to her horror, her eyes started to prickle. Why would that happen? She quickly closed her eyes so he couldn't see them fill.

"Look at me, Lily."

Rats. There they were naked on a huge chaise lounge with the sun shining on them and she was starting to cry. She opened her eyes and gave him a wide smile. "Yes?"

His brown gaze didn't miss a thing. She wondered if they trained him for that in foreign-aid school. "Do you have any regrets, Lily? I know this is a very sudden relationship, and neither of us has ever been with anyone else…like this."

She didn't answer, didn't know what to say, and his face tightened in concern. His muscles tensed as if he was about to get up.

"Wait!"

He rolled next to her, brushing her hair off her face.

"I, um…" she started. "It's not what you think. I was looking at you, and the sun was shining on you, and I thought how, um, wonderful it was to be here at this perfect time and perfect place." Geez, for a writer she was incredibly incoherent. Maybe because she preferred describing other people and their activities rather than open up her own emotions for scrutiny.

"Oh." Relief spread across his face. "As we talked about before—the moment where everything is exactly as it should be. The poet Baudelaire said to 'dream of sweetness,' where everything is rich, peaceful and sensual."

"That's it, exactly. I've never experienced that with a man." She fought back a blush at being so open, but, hey, she was already physically naked. A little bit of emotional nakedness wouldn't be out of place.

His eyes widened. "And you feel that with me?"

"Well, yes."

"And I have felt that with you—from the first time you bumped into me at the hostel."

"No." She narrowed her eyes at him. "You thought I had a terrible accent and was an obnoxious summer tourist."

"I did not. I thought you were a beautiful, cheerful American woman who took pity on a scruffy, rude backpacker and bought him breakfast."

"And look how well you cleaned up," she joked. "All for the price of a cup of coffee and a croissant."

"Did you call me cheap?" He placed his hand on his chest in mock dismay. "Cruel woman."

"Cruel man." He was the furthest thing from cruel, but he knew she was teasing him.

"What? And considering how hard I work to please you?"

"How can I ever make it up to you?" she purred, running her hand down his belly to cup his growing erection.

He thrust into her hand. "Surprise me."

She pushed him onto his back. "You're on." She swung her leg over his waist and straddled him.

"Ah, Lily." He grabbed her hips and helped her settle on him, his cock pushing inside her again. He cupped her breasts and played with her sensitized nipples, his big hands brown against her paler skin.

"My favorite bikini top." She smiled down at him.

He grinned. "If you have to wear anything, wear me."

"You wear me out." Her legs were starting to burn from moving up and down on him but she didn't care. "But in a good way."

"Poor Lily." His chest glistened with sweat and his hair was falling into ringlets at the edges. "I'll make it up to you, I promise." He caressed her clit and she leaned forward, bracing her hands on his shoulders.

His free hand cupped her bottom running up her back to the nape of her neck. "Kiss me, *ma belle* Lily."

She eagerly complied, opening her mouth to him as his tongue possessed her as thoroughly as his cock. She moaned and squirmed, her climax building. He slid his hand down to her bottom and massaged there. The double sensation of his hands in front and back was overwhelming and she bucked sharply on top of him.

He hummed low in his throat and kept it up until she arched and clutched at him. He quickly followed her over the edge and she collapsed onto him.

Jack rolled her onto the chaise and they kissed naked in the sun. "Not so shy anymore, eh, Lily?"

"Only with you." She nuzzled his neck.

"But of course." He gathered her into his arms. "And despite what you may think, I am only clothing-optional with you."

She laughed and pinched his firm buttock. "I know that—you have tan lines."

"And we are going to get burn lines if we don't get out of the sun." He stood and scooped her up as she squealed in surprise.

"Don't hurt yourself."

He scoffed and walked toward the house. "You are much lighter than some of the equipment Jean-Claude has me tote around."

"Don't let him work you too hard," she fretted.

He pinched her bottom and she yelped. "Oh, I work hard. A strong woman like you needs a strong man."

"You think I'm strong?" Lily hugged him closer.

He shook his head in mock dismay. "But if only you could be a little more docile instead of quizzing everything I say."

"Yes, milord." She fluttered her eyelashes.

"What?" He looked shocked at her joking acquiescence.

"Isn't that what all the French peasant girls say to the local nobleman who's offered to ravish them?"

He tipped back his head and roared with laughter. "And I am the local nobleman who has the right to ravish the peasant girls!" He nudged open the patio door with his foot. "I am luring you to my noble lair to have my way with you. How do you feel about a noble attempt at a bath in a hot tub?"

"Milord, lead the way."

14

LILY CAME DOWN to the kitchen early the next morning and found a note from Jack. "Lily, meet me at the lavender field up the hill. Bring coffee. Yours, Jack."

She smiled and set to brewing the milky *café au lait* she was coming to prefer. Once that was perking, she picked up his note and reread it. *Yours, Jack.* That was nice. Lily put great stock in words. She knew not everybody did, but Jack was a methodical, precise man and meant exactly what he said—and wrote.

She didn't expect him to sign it *Love, Jack* or *All my love, Jack,* so that word of affection was a pleasant surprise.

Once the coffee was done and poured into a battered steel thermos, she slung her camera around her neck and headed up the hill to the lavender field, her calves burning in a pleasant way as the gravel road crunched under her hiking boots.

The first field she came to was empty of blooms and workers. That made sense, since it had probably ripened first, being at a slightly lower and warmer elevation. Another quarter mile or so brought her to the field under harvest.

Lily stood at the edge, her gaze immediately drawn to Jack's chestnut head—and his bare torso. Her lips pursed. He was going to get sunburned if he wasn't careful. But he was a grown man and had worked in tropical areas with much more intense sun than France.

His muscles bunched under his skin as he stooped and clipped the wiry stems, setting them aside. He moved down the row and stopped at the end, straightening to stretch his back. Jean-Claude yelled at him, gesturing for Jack to get back to work. Jack replied in kind, causing the older man to bellow with laughter.

The other harvesters glanced up from their own rows and grinned, obviously used to the byplay between the two men. The farmworkers were a diverse lot, men and women both, young and old.

Lily set down the thermos and took several photos, the tableau reminding her of the popular bucolic nineteenth-century paintings of peasants gathering harvest.

But her lens kept swiveling back to Jack. Instead of the sleepy shepherd lad he'd resembled on the train, he looked like a pagan harvest god, powerful and fertile, ripening crops with his touch.

He had joined Jean-Claude on the side of the field and the two men had an intense discussion, pointing at the current field and then up the hill at what was probably the next one on the list. Jack was insisting on something and finally Jean-Claude tossed his hands up in the air and slapped him on the back.

Almost as if Jack were in charge…but he did know about lavender from his family's own farm. Then he spotted her and strode toward her, leaping the low stone fence surrounding the field with an easy jump.

"Good morning, *chérie*." Jack lifted the camera over her head, bent her over his arm and kissed her. His skin was hot velvet, warmed by the sun. She clutched his shoulders as he leisurely moved his mouth over hers.

She dimly became aware of the cheers and catcalls from the harvesters, and Jack planted a kiss on the tip of her nose. "Sorry, Lily. Farmwork brings out my earthy side," he murmured suggestively.

She blinked a couple of times. His "earthy side" had popped up in the bedroom, of course, but this public display of affection was new. She didn't mind, and in fact found it fascinating how life in Provence was healing him from the thin, tired man she'd first met in Paris.

The harvesters had returned to work after Jean-Claude's good-natured shout. Jack pulled on a T-shirt he'd tossed on the wall and took her hand.

"I have a surprise planned for this morning."

"Really?" More of a surprise than a kiss. "What kind of surprise?"

His eyes fell to the scoop-neck blouse showing the top curves of her breasts. "I forget."

Lily huffed in pretend exasperation. "Start remembering."

"Cruel woman." His brown puppy-dog eyes were almost enough to make her relent, but her natural curiosity won out.

"Jack…"

"All right, all right. Remember the perfume lab at the factory? You have an appointment with the 'nose,' the master perfumer, to make your own signature fragrance."

"Really?" She flung her arms around his neck and kissed his cheek. "I read about that online but didn't think I'd have the chance to do that. It doesn't cost too much, does it?"

He hugged her back. "Not at all. It is a popular tourist

outing and no trouble to arrange. We have time for coffee but not anything else," he said regretfully.

She handed him the thermos. "Drink up. I'll model my new perfume for you later."

"Your perfume and nothing else."

She giggled and soon they were in the little white car heading toward the village.

Jack parked near the perfume factory and they quickly found the perfume master, an elegant woman in her fifties with a gray-streaked blond bob and skin that would have looked great on a woman half her age. Probably kept out of the sun and had an inside track on wonderful botanical products.

Jack introduced them. "Simone Laurent is the best nose in the business. The House of Laurent is built on her skill."

"I'm so excited," Lily told her. "The world of perfume is fascinating, especially when you grow so many of your own ingredients right here in Provence."

Simone smiled. "We are indeed fortunate to have such a perfect climate for the flowers and plants—our own corner of paradise."

"I love it here." Lily squeezed Jack's hand. "The sun, the blue skies and hot, dry air. I'm from Philadelphia, and it's very humid there. Much of the city was built on a swamp. They even had the largest yellow-fever outbreak in American history."

Jack smiled. "Fortunately I've had my shots for that, so I will be safe."

Did that mean that he was coming to visit her there? Her heart gave a funny thump, and she smiled up at him. "The Liberty Bell is always a fun sight."

Simone was already leading them down the hall. "Come, come, we have work to do." She ushered them into a laboratory-type space with a large white desk and several dark brown glass bottles on shelves lining the walls. "This is the perfume laboratory. Nothing but the highest quality oils and essences for the House of Laurent." Simone pulled out a clipboard and paper. "We will write down your final choice and keep it on file. Whenever you need a new bottle, you can call us and we will mix it to order. Now tell me which fragrances you like and which you dislike."

Lily thought for a second. "Not roses." Mrs. Wyndham loved fresh roses in the house and she always associated that scent with her.

"Good." Simone made a note. "What else?"

"I like vanilla." The elderly pastry chef who'd preceded Stan had always made sugar cookies for Lily.

"A good, warm base."

"And in honor of my trip to Provence, I thought I could have some lavender in the blend."

"Lavender?" Simone smiled. "Excellent. We have the best lavender oil in the world here in Provence. And the best of the best comes from the de Brissard estate."

"Really?" She turned to Jack in excitement. "You're helping harvest the best lavender in the world. Doesn't that make you proud?"

"Hot and sweaty more than anything," he quipped. "But yes, we are undeniably proud of that lavender."

Simone grinned widely. "Family-owned since 1323. Isn't that correct, Jacques?"

Lily gasped in amazement. "That long. What a sense of history. Jack, maybe I should do a blog post on the de Brissard family."

He shifted from foot to foot. "I wouldn't bother. They have always been an extremely boring lot. But a blog post about Simone and the factory would be very interesting."

Simone smiled. "We are always looking for good publicity, especially to introduce our name and creations to North American buyers."

"I'm writing for *Fashionista Magazine*." It still sent a thrill through her to say that.

"Congratulations. My daughter enjoys that magazine. Me, I cannot read fashion magazines because of all the perfume samples mixing together. Overwhelming for a woman like me." She laughed and reached for a plain brown bottle. "But here we have the de Brissard lavender." She uncapped the bottle and dropped a couple drops of the oil on a paper strip about six inches long. She let it dry for a few seconds and handed it to Lily.

Lily took a cautious sniff and her head almost spun from the concentrated essence. She was immediately thrown back in time to their afternoon in the lavender field, the heat and sun and buzz of cicadas almost loud enough to drown the pounding of the blood in her ears. "Jack, it smells like those fields where we…toured the plants," she finished.

Simone gave her a knowing smile. "That is the power of scent. One wears it outwardly to communicate with others but it conjures the most personal and private memories to the wearer."

"Almost like a secret—I know something that you don't know."

Jack brushed her hair back over her shoulder, his fingers lingering on her collarbone. "The mystery of a woman. Inviting and intriguing to us poor men as we strive to discover the hidden depths."

Lily covered his hand with hers. "You men can be pretty mysterious yourselves."

Simone interjected, "Ah, but that is the wonder of life, eh?" She clapped her hands together. "Enough philosophy. Let's get to work."

For the next hour or so, Lily sniffed test strips until they all started to blend in her poor, untrained mind. She stepped outside a couple times to clear her head, but even the town smelled of flowers, so that didn't help much.

Finally, though, she and Simone had put something together that was floral but woodsy, sweet but exotic. "It's not quite there," she said in disappointment. "The lavender and vanilla are wonderful together along with the base of cedar, but it's missing something."

Simone smiled and dipped a paper tester strip into a bottle, adding it to the wand of papers. Lily cautiously sniffed and her cheeks pulled into a wide grin. "That's it!"

Jack leaned in for a sniff and nodded in approval. "Wonderful. Whatever did you add?"

The perfumer spread her hands wide. "Lily, of course. One cannot make perfume for Lily without any lilies."

They burst out laughing. Jack bent down and kissed Simone on the cheek. "Ah, Simone. The 'nose' knows, as they say."

"Always. Now, Jacques, we still have your cologne formula if you need a new bottle of it."

"You've done this before?" Lily didn't know why that would surprise her since he and Simone were obviously old friends.

"A long time ago, but no, Simone, I don't need any more fragrance."

The perfumer shook her head. "But, Jacques, you know that the oils start breaking down after about a year and quality suffers. Certainly you will not wear your old supply anymore?"

"Well…"

She scoffed. "If you do, don't you dare mention where you got it. I will not have people wondering why Jacques

Montford is wearing something of ours that smells like a Marseilles alley."

He sighed in exasperation and threw up his hands. "I promise to throw away that bottle if you will make me another."

"Bon." Simone smiled like the cat with the canary. "You know, Jacques, we should go into partnership. Put your fragrance into mass production and split the proceeds. We could call it—"

"Merci, but no."

Lily thought it sounded like a great idea. "But you could use the money, Jack. Especially since you've been ill and aren't working right now."

"What?" Simone eyed him from head to toe. "You've been sick?"

"I caught a bug overseas but I am much better now. And I *am* working—working for Jean-Claude."

"Well, that is certainly a switch. I hope you've been kind to him."

"Always." Jack smiled. "And Lily is getting all of Marthe-Louise's recipes."

"I wish—she probably knows several thousand." At the mention of food, Lily's stomach rumbled.

He pulled her to her feet. "Lunchtime, eh? Would you care to join us, Simone?"

"No, no." She waved her hand dismissively. "I must mix both bottles for you and besides, I would not want to intrude on your *tête-à-tête.*" She stood and kissed Lily first on both cheeks, then Jack. She clasped his hand for a second. "Please take care of yourself, Jacques. You are very important to all of us."

"As are you, Madame Simone." He gave a quick bow and kissed the back of her hand. "Mmm, you smell wonderful."

"Ah, Jacques, be gone." She waved him away, laughing. "Come back later for your *parfum.*"

Jack took Lily's hand and guided her out of the perfume lab. "Anything you want for lunch, it is yours."

She looked up at him in worry. "Jack, we have to stop this crazy spending. Custom perfume and fancy lunches must be cutting into your budget. At least let me help. Since we're staying at the guesthouse, I haven't used the money I planned for the hostels."

He wrapped his arm around her shoulder and guided her down the crowded sidewalk. "You are a generous woman, *chérie.* But don't worry about the money. I do still get my salary from the relief agency. I am on a medical leave, not unemployed. As you said, the guesthouse is free and I believe Marthe-Louise would slap me with a spoon if I offered her money for the meals she has been cooking for us."

"True." The housekeeper would be vastly insulted, even if they meant well.

"Now what would you like for lunch?"

"I would like...fresh mussels in a white wine sauce tossed with fresh pasta." Her stomach growled again. "Also a crusty loaf of bread to dip in the leftover sauce."

"Wonderful. There is this nearby café that gets shellfish fresh from the sea. The owner's nephew has a fishing boat and then sends the best to his uncle."

"Jack, you know the most fantastic places around here." She snuggled into his side. "And after lunch, we'll pick up the perfume and model it for each other later."

"Sounds delightful."

Lily smiled in satisfaction. Perfume, pasta and Jack— but definitely not in that order. Life couldn't get any better.

JACK LEFT A sleeping Lily, the fragrance of their mingled cologne and perfume still scenting the air of their bedroom.

He was still dishonest with Lily. His stomach churned, and he couldn't even blame the shellfish.

He was a forthright man—why had he started this deception? Had his experience with Nadine so jaded him that he thought every woman was out to snag a rich man, a titled man?

His only title should have been "Loser." Lily was nothing like Nadine—and that was good. But he needed advice, so he pulled on a pair of shorts and picked up his phone. He stopped in the kitchen for a bottle of water and walked out to the pool.

Jack sat heavily into a cushioned chair and turned on his phone. It immediately signaled a new text message from the coordinator at the relief agency, asking how he was feeling. Apparently there was a volcanic eruption in Malaysia and they needed a doctor. Not for anything long-term, she assured him. Just long enough to set up a clinic in the refugee camps and take care of immediate needs.

He touched the reply screen. He should go—they needed him. But then he stopped. Maybe he should get some advice.

He dialed another number instead. "Hi, Frank, it's Jack."

"Jack!" Frank sounded delighted. "How are you? Enjoying the sun?"

He stretched his legs out in the sun. Still rather skinny and pale. "The weather here is wonderful."

"Ah yes, I remember from that one summer we worked the lavender harvest," Frank reminisced. "And those beautiful French girls sure enjoyed how nice we smelled, didn't they?"

Jack grunted in agreement. One particular woman and her perfume were what had put him into this strange mood.

"You find anyone to share the sun and lavender with you?"

Jack sighed heavily. "Yes. And I think I may have royally screwed up."

There was a moment of silence. "Uh-oh. We'd better call George for this one."

In a minute, George was on the line.

Frank minced no words. "George, Jack is in trouble."

"What's wrong, Jack? Are you still sick?" George asked in alarm.

"No, I feel much better. It's just—" He broke off his sentence, not knowing what he was trying to say.

"Go ahead and tell us the details. It's about a *woman,*" he stage-whispered to George. He had always been Mr. Fix-It, leaping in to help whenever he could.

"Let the man think, Frank." George sounded amused. He well could afford to be, having gone through his own struggles with the female sex earlier in the spring.

"I *can't* think, that's the problem. I can only think about—about Lily, this woman I just met last week. I can't sleep unless I'm next to her. I can't be away from her without wondering where she is, if she's enjoying herself, if people are being kind to her..." he wound down, verbally if not mentally.

"Jack, Jack," George soothed. "It's okay. You've had a rough few months stuck off in Asia. No wonder you're attracted to the first pretty face that came along."

"Pretty face?" For the first time in his life, Jack wished he could hit George. "Lily is smart, beautiful, talented, witty—not just a pretty face," he spit out.

After a few seconds of tense silence, Frank cleared his throat. "George didn't mean it that way, Jack. She sounds great, she really does."

"Well, she is."

"I am sorry, Jack. I didn't know you felt that way about her," George apologized.

"What way?" he demanded. Another awkward silence. Jack realized he was totally losing his grip. Chewing out his best friends, for crying out loud, letting a woman come between them?

Frank jumped in again, hating to see them argue. "George and I are glad you met somebody nice. Does she like Provence?"

Glad for a more neutral topic, Jack readily said, "Oh, she can't get enough of the landscape and the food, but it's really the people that fascinate her. I spend hours translating for her with all her questions about how they grow lavender, what their mangy hunting dogs are named, how many children they have, anything at all."

"Well, that sounds promising," George said. "You're tied to the land, like we are. Any woman you are serious about would have to understand the pros and cons of you being the Comte de Brissard."

"That's my problem. I haven't told her who I am."

There was another second of silence. "She doesn't know?" Frank asked in amazement. "But you're staying at your own home, harvesting your own lavender and roaming your own estate. She must think you're the biggest moocher in France—the houseguest from hell."

"Really, Frank," George chided him. "I'm sure Jack had his reasons for portraying himself as a simple disaster-relief physician."

"She doesn't know I'm a doctor, either," he mumbled.

Frank guffawed. "You've really stepped in the cow patties now." Frank had always loved American farming colloquialisms. "Your only hope is to tell her the truth—and pronto, before someone else does."

"I have to agree with him, Jack. It sounds as if you've been less than forthcoming. And especially if you like her, and she likes you. It sounds as if you have much in common—both the adventurous types and you both like Provence."

"Like? Aside from the language, it's as if she were a native. Lily loves it here."

The L-word hung significantly over them. Lily loved his homeland. What else did Lily love? She couldn't love... him, could she?

No, of course not. Why would she love him? He was a skinny, pasty Frenchman who knew too much about dying and not enough about living. "Another thing just came up. The agency wants me to go to Malaysia. Just short-term," he hastily added. "I haven't told them my answer yet."

The air of disapproval was palpable. "I know what you can tell them," Frank announced. "You can tell them you almost died earlier in the year and they can go to hell."

George cleared his throat. "I have to agree with Frank, though not quite as bluntly. What would you say to a patient who wanted to do the same thing? You'd keep them home for much longer, wouldn't you?"

"Yes, but they need me."

"So do we, Jack," said George.

"You guys are fine. This farm runs well without me. My mother is tied up in her social events. I'd be at loose ends if I didn't have someone to help."

Frank made a sound of exasperation. "We all need to be needed. You don't have to become a martyr for it."

It was as if someone had chopped him in the gut. Nadine had said almost the same thing to him at his disastrous homecoming party. Had called him St. Jacques and told him he wanted a statue to himself. "Guys, I have to go."

"Oh. Right," Frank said hesitantly. "Take care of yourself, okay?"

"Yes, please do," echoed George. "And again, accept

my apologies in casting aspersions on your ladyfriend. I misspoke."

Jack accepted, of course, feeling grumpy and irritable and generally pissed off—at himself, not George.

Jack hung up. He could go to Malaysia without having some kind of martyr-complex. His friends just didn't understand the shortage of willing doctors. Jack should know better than to get all worked up over trivialities. After all, he was the cool, collected Dr. Montford, trained physician, award-winning philanthropist—and all-around jerk to his friends.

"Did he hang up, George?"

"I believe so, Frank."

"He's a goner for this girl, George."

"I think you're right, Frank."

"I usually am."

"Ha."

"Ha, yourself. Go give Renata a kiss for me."

"*Ciao*, Frank."

"*Ciao*, George."

15

LILY FINISHED HER blogpost for *Fashionista Magazine* and checked the clock again. Jack had been working outdoors for several hours and she hoped he wasn't overdoing it. Maybe he was back at the manor house with Marthe-Louise. Her stomach growled. And if not, maybe there was something to eat there.

Lily wandered down to the kitchen garden. Tomatoes, herbs and various squash overflowed the beds. Mrs. Wyndham's gardener would be pea-green with envy. He fought humid weather and various related plant ailments all summer. Marthe-Louise was stooping over to clip some chives. "Ah, *bonjour,* Lily. You desire Jacques?"

Heck yes, she desired him, but probably not what Marthe-Louise meant since even Lily knew the French verb to want in a generic sense was *désirer.* Her cheeks heated. "*Oui.* Where is he?" She mimicked searching for him and Marthe-Louise laughed.

"The lavender, it is ready. Men working together in field."

Ooh la la. The memory of Jack, a sweaty field hand, stripped to the waist was hot. Maybe she could see him from the side of the house that had a view of the hills. "Can

I…" She gestured at the doorway leading to the formal living area of the manor.

Marthe-Louise waved her on. "Go. I cook nice dinner, eh?"

"Good." She smiled at the older woman. She and Jack would have to get her a fancy gift before they left. Cooking for them all the time was above and beyond what she had expected.

Lily had asked Jack when the de Brissard family would return, but he said the lady of the house preferred Paris and probably wouldn't be back this summer. Lily had no idea why not. She'd enjoyed Paris but loved Provence.

Lily walked down the hallway past the dining room and turned into the formal living room, or salon. Undoubtedly this was used for parties and maybe even weddings, being able to hold over a hundred people by her calculations.

She peered out the large French doors leading to the stone terrace, but no sight of Jack in the lavender fields. Maybe they were farther up the hill. She turned and caught sight of a large framed photograph hung on the wall that hadn't been there during her tour. She would have remembered it because Jack was the subject.

Her eyebrows shot up as she peered closely at it. Jack in some fancy tux and tails, with a red sash across his chest, complete with a large gold sunburst medal pinned to it. And there was a woman in the photo. Unless Jack had a thing for older women with hair the same shade of auburn as him, she was his mom.

Lily looked closer and found several similarities in their high cheekbones, strong jaw and wavy hair. His mom was dressed just as fancily in a copper silk dress with a full skirt, and she was seated on an elaborate French-style chair upholstered in white and trimmed in gold. Jack stood behind her, his hand on her shoulder.

Pieces of the puzzle were starting to fit together, and she had the feeling it wouldn't be a cute puppy puzzle or panoramic lavender field jigsaw.

Lily went back into the kitchen. "Marthe-Louise?" she called.

"Oui?" The housekeeper came out from the butler's pantry, wiping her hands on a white towel.

"Photo." Lily jerked her thumb backward at the salon. *"Grand* photo."

The guilty look on Marthe-Louise's face confirmed her suspicion. When Jack had brought her for the tour, he'd sent Marthe-Louise in there first to take down the evidence that he *owned* all of this.

Not only was he probably ten times richer than Mrs. Wyndham back in Philly, but he owned a huge chunk of France, the farm, this giant house plus the guesthouse. Where he had pretended to be a guest.

"Marthe-Louise." Her tone was harsher than she had planned and Marthe-Louise shrank back. Lily took a breath. "What is Jack's real name?"

The older woman frowned. "Jacques Charles Olivier Fortanier Montford. Comte de Brissard."

De Brissard. The lavender family. *"Comte?"* She'd never heard that name before.

"In English, *count*. His mother is the Dowager Countess de Brissard."

Lily made a choking noise. "Royalty?" That jerk. He had said the de Brissards were a dull lot, and not to bother writing about them. No wonder.

"Oh, no." The older lady chuckled, relieved to give Lily some good news for once. "Nobility."

"Oh, is that all?" Lily gave an appalled laugh. "Good grief. I should have been curtsying before getting into bed with him."

Marthe-Louise had caught the gist of Lily's statement and pulled her wide cheeks back in a nervous grin. "Ah, the food—it burns." She scurried away before Lily could say that it didn't smell like anything was even cooking.

The mythical food wasn't the only thing burning—so was Lily's temper. She glared at the photo of the lying Comte de Brissard and stalked through the kitchen and out the back door.

She hit the stone pathway leading from the kitchen garden to the guesthouse.

Jack was walking shirtless down the hill from the lavender fields, wiping his face with a cloth, bits of lavender blossom and twigs stuck to his chest and back. "Ah, *chérie,* there you are. Did you get a lot accomplished this afternoon? I hope so, because I have plans for *you* this evening."

He smelled of lavender and sun and heat. Yummy. She tamped down any wayward twinges of desire. She was mad at him and had to remember that. "Hello, Your Royal Highness."

"Oh." He stopped. "Lily, I was going to tell you, but the time was never right and then…" He tried to hug her but she pushed him away.

"Forget it! You can go be a sweaty field hand for all I care. I never thought it was such a hot look anyway."

"What?" He raised his eyebrows. "It *is* hot outside."

"Never mind!" Lily tapped her foot. "Any other secrets I should know about?"

He looked away guiltily.

"Oh, *milord,* now what? Are you next in line for the French throne?"

"I wouldn't take that job for a million euros. Look what happened to Louis the Sixteenth." He laughed but quickly became serious at her cold gaze. "Nothing so glamorous.

My training for disaster-relief work is in medicine. I'm a physician. They want me to go to Malaysia, but I told them no this morning. I'm staying in Provence."

Lily exhaled a long breath and slowly circled him.

He stared at her warily, craning his head over his shoulders. "What is it?"

"Looking for either a halo or a superhero cape."

"Lily…" He held out his hands to her.

"No wonder you knew the names of all those tropical diseases. You probably teach a course in that stuff."

"Some seminars at the tropical medicine institute in Paris," he admitted.

"A professor, as well. And yet you have time to chat with the rest of us mere mortals. How ever do you do it?"

He set his jaw. "And you wonder why I don't tell everyone about my background?"

"I am *everyone*. That's really nice."

"You know what I mean. You're more than that."

"So you should have told me. Madame Finch should have told me."

"I asked her not to. I wanted you to get to know the real me, and I wasn't sure if you'd be thrilled or repulsed at my circumstances."

"Lots of gold diggers?"

"Another entirely appropriate American saying." He took her hand, but she let her arm dangle loosely. "But I knew from the beginning that you weren't like that. In fact, from what you said, you didn't care for rich men anyway. I was afraid you would lump me in with them and not see me for myself."

"I would have seen you for yourself," she protested.

He shook his head. "What if I had said, 'I am the Comte de Brissard, physician and nobleman. Come to my luxurious villa in Provence where I can woo you with my worldly riches'?"

Lily automatically made a face and he pounced. "You see? That would have been your honest reaction and that would have been the end of any possibilities between us."

She considered her gut reaction and admitted he was probably right. "But that doesn't mean you should have waited until I found out. You could have told me you were a doctor when we talked about infectious diseases. And you could have told me you owned this whole place when we first came here."

"I know, *mon coeur,* and I am so sorry. My only excuse is selfishness. I did not want to risk having you leave me before we got to know each other, but I should have been up-front and honest with you as soon as possible."

"Yes, you should have." But she wasn't so angry anymore. "And I'm actually more impressed with your education. You had to earn that, not inherit it."

"Exactly." He smiled in relief. "I am not ashamed of my heritage, but the title of Comte de Brissard would have fallen to me if I were the biggest idiot in France. But being a physician, that is my real accomplishment." He tugged her closer. "And that is why I appreciate your hard work, as well. You are a writer, an entrepreneur. You are not relying on any family wealth or connections to succeed."

"Oh, Jack." She blushed a bit but rallied. "No more secrets." She started to shake her finger at him but instead started picking lavender bits off his firm, sweaty chest.

"I promise." He leaned down to kiss her but she turned away at a sudden loud engine noise. "What is that?"

Jack's eyes bugged out. "Oh, no."

"What?"

"Look, promise me you'll take the next ten minutes with a grain of salt."

"Oh, come on, are we in a soap opera? If you have an evil twin or are getting over amnesia, I swear I'm leaving right now. I knew I should have looked you up on Google, but you said you kept yourself off the internet."

"As much as possible, but you would have gotten several hits." The engine got louder, traveling along in a cloud of dust so Lily couldn't see what was coming.

"Grrr." Lily felt like kicking herself. Crack Reporter-Girl had fallen down on the job.

A big silver Rolls-Royce pulled up in the driveway, looking exactly like the old TV ad. The window rolled down, but instead of a distinguished gray-haired gent asking for American-made French-style mustard, the middle-aged, *very* well-preserved Frenchwoman whom she'd seen in the family photo gave them a startled look before stepping out of the car. Lily dropped his hand.

She kissed him on both cheeks, skillfully avoiding his damp skin, then scolding him. "Oh, Jacques."

"Oh, *Maman,*" he groaned. Lily was so shocked by everything that was happening that she almost missed the fashionable blonde sliding out from the backseat.

Almost. "If that's Jack's mother, then who are you?" Lily asked. "His sister?"

The blonde gave what might be called a tinkling laugh by writers more twee and fanciful than Lily, and Lily disliked her immediately. "Don't be ridiculous. I'm Nadine, his fiancée."

Lily's dislike for the blonde turned to hate. And Jack the Count wasn't far behind.

"WAIT!" JACK BELLOWED, seeing Lily sprint up the hill toward the guesthouse. His mother deftly blocked him as if she were some kind of American football linesman and he had to stutter-step past her. "*Maman,* please get out of my way."

"Jacques, we just got here. Nadine found your photo online on *Fashionista Magazine* and we recognized the birthmark on the back of your neck right away. Whoever that girl is who is calling you Pierre in her blog, she certainly is temperamental. Standing here shouting at you and then running away. Not very dignified, if I may say so."

"Forget about dignified, *Maman.* What are you doing here? What is Nadine doing here?"

"Making sure you're all right." She lowered her voice. "Nadine says the dysentery can affect your brain." The last word came out in a horrified whisper.

Damn Nadine for scaring his mother. "Dysentery affects your guts, not your brain, and besides, where did Nadine go to medical school anyway?"

"You know I'm concerned about you, Jacques." She made as if to embrace him but realized he had dead plant matter all over his sticky skin. Lily would have hugged him anyway if she'd thought he had a brain disease. Nadine would probably welcome a bit of brain damage in him, preferably in his frontal lobe to destroy his long-term memory of all the crappy things she'd done to him.

He gave her a hard look and ran after Lily. She was moving at a good clip, but he caught up to her when she slowed for a corner. "Lily, wait!"

She spun to face him. "Another woman, and you didn't think to mention this, either." She gave him a disappointed stare. "What did I do to you to deserve this?" She gestured at the house. "Not trusting me to tell me who you actually are. And after I was so careful to keep you anonymous in my blog. Apparently I could have made much more money by revealing your true identity to one of the tabloids and giving them all the inside gossip."

"I wanted you to like me for myself. And we're not engaged anymore."

"Right. I bet if I went on Google, I could find your engagement announcement."

"Yes, but—"

"Weak, weak, weak!" she blurted.

"It's the truth."

"And," she continued as if she hadn't heard him, "not only do you have a fiancée, but she's an upperclass blonde bitch. Well, at least she was pretty bitchy to me, but then again, I'd be bitchy to a woman who I was pretty sure was sleeping with my husband-to-be."

She turned her back to him and stalked in the door of the guesthouse.

"She's not my—!" Jack was distracted suddenly by the Rolls rolling up the driveway. The blonde bitch popped out. "Go away, Nadine."

"This heat is bothering your mother. She was feeling faint, so I left her on that cute bench in front of the house."

"What? Did you at least get her a glass of water? Is she going to pass out and hit her head on the stone?"

Nadine widened her eyes as if she'd never considered any consequences to her actions, which she probably hadn't. "My goodness, Jacques, maybe we should get back down to her. Marthe-Louise won't know what to do if your mother goes into heat shock."

"Heat stroke," he corrected automatically. "I'll have Marthe-Louise mix her some homemade rehydration solution." But Lily was in the guesthouse, upset and hurting. He ran in the door and shouted her name.

"Go away, Jack!" she shouted. It sounded like she was upstairs.

"Lily, my mother needs me—wait for me." Nadine was

tugging on his arm so he left, casting an anguished look upstairs.

"Here, take the Rolls," Nadine told him. "I'll walk down in a minute." His ex bundled him into the car and he directed the chauffeur to take him to the manor house.

He'd fix up his mother and then he'd fix up his mess with Lily.

"LILY?" A FEMALE French voice called her name.

Lily came out from the bedroom and peered over the railing. Nadine stood in the foyer staring up at her with a pitying glance. If there was anything Lily hated in the world more than humiliation, it was pity. She took the offensive. "So you're Jack's fiancée."

"Jack?" She gave that nerve-grating laugh again. "Ah, Jacques and that American phase he went through."

Lily squeezed the railing hard, not liking the idea that she was a continuation of his "American phase," whatever that had been. "He never mentioned you." That was the closest she could come to apologizing for inadvertently committing premarital adultery.

Nadine shrugged and climbed the stairs, Lily's stomach falling with every step. "Jacques and I have a different relationship than you are accustomed to." She reached the top landing and stood eye to eye with Lily.

Next to the Frenchwoman's perfectly tailored cream-colored linen pants, white T-shirt and French designer silk scarf knotted chicly around her neck, Lily's own outfit fell sadly short—cutoff khaki shorts and pink tourist T-shirt with a big black camera and strap silk-screened on it that she'd bought for herself as a gag gift.

But she tried to rally. She was not the high school's token poor girl anymore. "What kind of relationship *do* you have?"

Nadine smiled gently. "Jacques was not himself when he came back from Borneo."

"Burma," Lily corrected. Geez, didn't she know what country in which he'd been deathly ill? "And you didn't fly out to be with him when he was so sick?"

Shock and disgust flared in her crystal-blue eyes but she quickly dampened it. "I didn't have all my immunizations, and I knew Jacques wouldn't want me to become ill, as well."

"Hmmph." Lily would have risked it.

"He needed space and a way to, how to say it? Blow off steam." She gave Lily a meaningful look. "I knew very well what he might do once out here in the country. He gets the physical appetites of a peasant."

Ah, and Lily was the peasant pressure release valve. Did Nadine *not* like "blowing off steam" with Jack? Was she nuts? Or as cold in bed as she seemed outside of it? "Look, I don't know how the French nobility does things, but you don't seem very upset that he has cheated on you."

"Men do what they must." Catching the doubt in Lily's eyes, she raised her eyebrows. "But perhaps you doubt me? I *am* here with his mother, after all."

Lily pursed her lips.

"You would like proof we are engaged? You of course may ask Jacques himself, if you are inclined to a messy and upsetting conversation." She pulled her phone out of her purse and pressed it a few times. "Here is our engagement photo."

Lily unwillingly looked at the small digital display. Yes, it was Jacques in that formal tux-and-tails outfit, complete with sash across his chest, tastefully embracing Nadine, dressed in an ice-blue satin ballgown.

"And here is the notice of our engagement in the Paris newspaper." She typed for a minute and brought up a newspaper webpage written in French, of course, but their names and the words *fiancé, fiancée* and *le mariage* were mentioned several times.

There it was in black-and-white on the web. She cleared her throat. "And you still want to marry him despite the fact he cheated on you?" This didn't make sense. Jack was scrupulously honest.

Except that he had lied about what he did for a living, lied about his real name and lied about his family owning a good chunk of Provence.

So much for scrupulously honest. She shook her head. Had she ever really known him?

Nadine waved her nicely manicured hand—French-manicured, of course. "We will, naturally, have much to discuss. But I am a forgiving woman. Jacques already told me about you. He said you are trying to be a writer."

"I try." Nadine needed to leave before Lily biffed her.

"Jacques says someday if you get lucky, you may be able to get a real writing job."

"He said that?" That really stung. Her blog and the articles for the *Fashionista Magazine* website wouldn't earn the Nobel Prize for Literature, but, dammit, she wrote carefully and put a lot of effort into them.

"Although every tourist who comes to France dabbles in travel writing, you were luckier than most and found your own personal tour guide."

"Right. But I think my tour is over."

"Good, I had hoped you will understand that he and I need some time together." Nadine gazed meaningfully at the open bedroom door, which showed Lily's clothes tossed on a chair.

"I understand." Lily headed into the bedroom, blinking hard.

Nadine followed her. Why didn't she back off and leave

Lily alone? She'd go as soon as she could pack. But how would she leave? They were in the country, several miles from the nearest train station. "I'll have to get a ride to the train." Not that she wanted to run into Jack, rather *Jacques,* again.

"The driver will take you," Nadine quickly offered. "You can ride in the Rolls-Royce. You will like it, your first ride in a Rolls."

Lily didn't bother to tell her she used to ride in one to school if Mrs. Wyndham was out of town. "Fine. Now, if you don't mind…"

Nadine made a graceful gesture and wafted out of the room, her heels clicking on the steps.

Lily chucked her clothes into her suitcase and grabbed her toiletries. She spotted the lavender perfume from the Count de Brissard's special AOC fields and dropped the bottle into the wastebasket. That kind of souvenir she didn't need.

Her shredded heart was enough.

16

JACK'S MOTHER WAS nowhere in sight as the Rolls dropped him off. He ran into the manor-house kitchen. "Marthe-Louise, where is my mother?"

She looked up from her pots and pans, startled. "What?"

"My mother. Where is she?"

Marthe-Louise gestured upstairs. "In her rooms. She said she was feeling the heat…."

Jack headed upstairs two at a time. "*Maman, Maman,* are you ill?"

There was no answer at her door, so he opened it. His mother was stretched out on her bed with a wet washcloth on her forehead. He crossed the wide room to put one hand on her forehead and the other around her wrist to check her pulse.

She lifted the cloth and stared at him. "Jacques, what are you doing?"

"Nadine said you were getting heat exhaustion."

"What?" She batted his hands away and he'd noticed she'd changed into a lightweight caftan, or muumuu, or whatever they called it. "I always get a touch of the heat when I am forced to come to the South in the middle of the summer."

Jacques decided not to point out she regularly came to the Riviera that time of year, but probably the sea breezes and glamour helped.

"Marthe-Louise gave me a cool drink and sent me upstairs to rest. But heat exhaustion?" She gave a tiny laugh, covering her eyes again. "Don't be ridiculous. And what are you doing with that American girl?" She laughed again. "Never mind, if you and Nadine have an agreement, it is none of your *maman's* business."

Jacques shook his head. "*Maman,* Nadine and I have no agreement because we are not engaged anymore."

She sat upright, the cloth falling onto her mouth. She tossed it aside impatiently. "What?"

"*Maman,* I told you we broke up before I left for Burma."

She waved her hand impatiently. "She told me that was a lovers' spat."

He shook his head. "I won't tell you all the details, but Nadine cheated on me. I caught her."

She stared at him with narrowed blue eyes. "She did?"

"*Oui.* I didn't want to tell you because…"

"Because you were terribly hurt."

Jack shrugged, lifting his hands in a helpless gesture. More relieved than hurt once the shock had worn off, but still…

"Jacques! Always when you are hurt you are crawling away to lick your wounds in private." She puffed in exasperation. "And you do not think to tell your poor *maman?* I invite that *salope* to your party. Oh, *mon dieu,* no wonder you run away. Your poor heart, it was broken, and to find the cause of it standing in your own home." She threw back her head in an anguished gesture.

"Really, I am fine now…."

"And now that you have found *l'amour* again with the

American girl— She isn't a bimbo you picked up, is she, Jack?"

He shook his head, trying to stifle a startled snicker at Lily being called a bimbo.

"Now that you have found love," his mother continued, "your own mother brings the lying piece of trash who broke your heart back into your country home. Ah!" She clutched at the breast of her muumuu, or caftan. "How can you ever forgive me?"

"I forgive you, *Maman*," he answered truthfully. His mother may have been a drama queen, but she was sincere in her efforts.

She cast away the wet cloth and jumped out of bed. Jack followed her. "Where is that awful girl? Nadine? Nadine?" She descended the stairs, shouting for his ex. Nadine appeared from the salon with a fashion magazine, having wisely decided to stay away from the kitchen, a pissed-off Marthe-Louise and her collection of sharp utensils.

"Oh, madame, you're feeling better. Jacques and I were worried that the heat was making you sick."

"You better worry about yourself, *ma petite.*" It wasn't an endearment. "How dare you lie to me—twice—about being affianced to my son? After what you did to him, with whomever you did it." His mother looked at him for more information but he shook his head.

His mother continued, obviously disappointed at the lack of details. "He is a good and brave man who deserves a decent woman, and you are not the woman for him. Get out!" She flung her arm to point to the front door.

Jack was torn between the desire to clap at her stage-worthy (but genuine) performance as Outraged Mother and the desire to get back to the guesthouse and smooth things over with Lily. Option two won. "*Maman*, you deal with her. I have to talk with Lily."

Nadine gave him a half smile. "Oh, I'm sorry. She left."

"Lily left?" He seriously considered throttling Nadine. "What did you say to her?"

"We chatted." Her half smile pulled into a smirk. "She decided she wanted to return to Paris. I suppose the slow, rural pace wasn't to her liking."

"That's not true," he snapped. "She loves it here—loves Provence, loves the lavender farm."

"Obviously not, or she would have stayed," she answered.

"And how did Lily leave?"

"The Rolls." Nadine started to get defensive as she realized how angry he was getting. "She insisted. She said she wasn't going to stick around this dusty, hot place in the middle of nowhere and wanted to hurry back to Paris. I think she wanted to shop for clothes." She wrinkled her nose. "She certainly needs some help in that area."

Now he knew she was lying. Lily hadn't bothered to shop much when she was in Paris the first time, preferring to concentrate on the people and sights. "You better hope the chauffeur unloaded your luggage because you're taking the train back to Paris, not Lily. Now do as my mother says and get out. You and I are going to the local train station."

"Jacques, wait!" his mother called.

"No, *Maman,* I've waited too long to meet someone like Lily, and I'm not going to wait any longer."

His mother gave him a sweet smile. "Nor should you, my treasure. But you need a shirt, do you not?"

"Oh." He glanced down at his bare chest, still damp with lavender florets stuck here and there. He pounded upstairs to his rarely used boyhood room. "Nadine, you better really hope she's still there, or…or…I'll think of something nasty."

He yanked open a drawer in his dressing room and

grabbed the first T-shirt he found, pulling it over his head. It was snug since he'd filled out quite a bit since he'd last worn his scouting jamboree shirt, but he didn't care.

He ran down the stairs and found his mother nose to nose with Nadine.

"My son may be nice, but I am not. If you have driven this Lily away, you can be sure that I will ruin you."

For the first time, Nadine started to look worried. His mother continued, "You may as well move to Burma because you will never get invited anywhere, you will sit behind a column at the opera house and you will never, *ever* get your photo in the society page again. What is the English term for that, Jacques?"

"Blackball?"

"Yes, how appropriate. Social *death*," Maman hissed. "And you know I will do it."

Nadine was pale and quivering by then. Jack rolled his eyes. He couldn't imagine Lily even caring about those things, as long as they were together.

"Go, go." His mother flapped her arms at them. "And you—*don't* come back," she told Nadine.

JACK GRIPPED THE steering wheel of the small rental car, Nadine's luggage stuffed to the ceiling and jammed into the trunk. Lily hadn't answered her phone, so he was racing to catch her in person.

Nadine sat next to him, her arms crossed over her chest. Their trip had been rather predictable, first filled with begging and pleading, then accusations and insults and finally a sullen silence that he welcomed.

He slowed down as he reached the village, driving as quickly as was safe over the narrow streets, which were still made of stone in parts. He stopped in front of the nineteenth-century train station and jumped out, dodging old ladies with their market baskets and tourists with maps.

"What about me?" Nadine screeched.

He pointed to the large timetable posted. "Get a ticket because you're not staying here."

He ran to the ticket office. "When did the last train leave?"

The older man inside checked the clock. "It has been two hours."

"Good." He sagged in relief. Lily had to be somewhere around here. "When does the next train leave?"

"For where, monsieur?"

"Anywhere."

"The train to Avignon leaves in ten minutes."

Jack thanked him and moved away, scanning the small crowd gathering to board. If she got to Avignon, he wouldn't be able to catch up. The high-speed train would take her to Paris in a few hours, and hundreds of flights left Paris every day.

If Lily had left France, he would follow her to Philadelphia. He would follow her to the ends of the earth—after all, he knew his way around them by now.

17

LILY STOOD ON the train platform, the French conversations buzzing around her like the cicadas in the lavender fields of the great de Brissard family. Damn Jack. Her mother's words about unexpected heartbreak from a nice man had been prophetic. It just showed that only a person you trusted could betray you so painfully.

Her backpack weighed on her shoulders as if she had bricks in it, but she knew it was the weight of her disappointment and sadness. When was that dumb train coming? If she had to stand around much longer, she'd either scream or burst into tears. Or both.

"Lily, Lily! Wait!" Jack sprinted toward her.

"Go away." Her voice quivered a bit on the last syllable.

"Lily, don't cry."

She pulled off her sunglasses to show him her dry, extremely angry eyes. "I am not crying. I haven't cried over anything but babies and puppies for years. Certainly not *men*."

"Nadine is a liar."

"Apparently she is also lazy." Lily spotted the blonde bitch standing next to the rental car, halfheartedly tugging at a small carry-on bag while she looked around for some unsuspecting male idiot to save her. Well, welcome to the real world, sister. No man was going to ride up on his white horse to make everything all right. Or drive up in a white rental car.

"I was engaged to her, it's true. But that ended abruptly right before I left for Burma when I found her with another man. In our bed."

Lily winced. Even though she was mad at Jack, it was an appalling image, even more appalling than the image in front of her. "Good grief, what on earth are you wearing?"

He looked down at himself. The red cotton looked spray-painted on, several inches of abdomen showing between his waistline and his T-shirt hem. It looked as if he had borrowed it from a thirteen-year-old. "My scout T-shirt from when I went to the big jamboree."

She peered at the silk-screened date. "Fifteen years ago?"

He shrugged. "I've filled out a bit since then. It was the first shirt I could find upstairs."

"You had plenty of shirts at the guesthouse."

His brown eyes darkened. "I couldn't waste a single minute getting to you."

Lily's traitorous heart thawed the tiniest bit but fought it. Stay strong, she told herself. "What do you want, Jack?"

"You."

She scoffed. "Well, duh. I know you want me. You couldn't keep your hands off me."

"Not just that, my Lily. I want you—all of you—forever."

"Not forever. I'm a summer fling. Nadine said so."

"You yourself said she was a liar."

Lily bit her lip. "So are you."

"Lying to you has been the biggest mistake of my life."

She narrowed her eyes, trying to judge his sincerity. But what was she thinking? She had to get away, get out of France.

Where was that freaking train?

Jack held out his hand. "Please, Lily. Come back with me. No more secrets. You can meet my mother and she can tell you every embarrassing thing that ever happened to me and every shameful mistake I've ever made."

"I can't stay until Christmas, you know." The quip slipped out before she remembered she was still furious with him.

He laughed but quickly turned serious. "You could, you know."

She shrugged. "And do what?"

"Stay with me. Marry me," he blurted.

"What?" she shrieked. He had some nerve. Her first marriage proposal was not in a fancy restaurant with a bottle of champagne and a diamond ring in a black velvet box. Instead, she was in a crowded, smelly French train station getting a throwaway desperation proposal from a man she wanted to hate, a man who lied to her, a man who wore a fifteen-year-old scout jamboree T-shirt.

He looked as shocked as she was but rallied. "Yes, yes, I mean it. Marry me, Lily."

They were drawing a crowd. No doubt thanks to Jack's local celebrity status.

Lily spotted a wooden bench tucked into an alcove and headed for it. "Get over here."

He followed, and when she spun to face him, he had a big grin on his face. "What are you smiling about?"

"You and me."

"There is no 'you and me,'" she informed him. "There is a Lily Adams and there is a Count Jacques Montford."

"You could be my countess," he said enticingly.

"Ack! And be called 'milady Lily'? It sounds like a brand of bras."

"You could start one if you wanted."

"Stop, all right? Stop trying to bribe me with noble titles, lavender farms and bra companies."

"What, then? What can I bribe you with?"

Himself. But she didn't say that out loud. Or did she? His grin disappeared.

"Myself?"

Crap.

"Isn't that what I said?" she decided to bluff.

"Yes. And actually, that is why I portrayed myself as a plain aid worker in a borrowed guesthouse. Because I am not accustomed to people looking beyond the trappings of my life and judging me for myself."

"Right. Because everyone is so shallow they can't separate you from your money."

He shrugged. "Society can be that way. You grew up in it. Didn't you know people like that?"

"Yes. But you had plenty of chances to come clean with me once you knew me—and you didn't." That was the part that upset her the most. "I told you all about my childhood."

"Not all. Why do you dislike people with property, people with some money? Was she unkind to you, the lady your mother works for?"

"Her? No." Lily looked away, not wanting to discuss it.

"Who?" he prodded.

She set her jaw. "I survived the prep school, all right? I was almost out of there but got a crush on one of the rich, good-looking guys my senior year. He invited me to prom, I was over the moon, and he saw stars when he tried to convince me forcefully to sleep with me after the dance."

Jack took a step toward her. A muscle in his cheek twitched.

"Fortunately for me, I grew up working hard and lifting heavy objects. And our gardener had studied in Japan and taught me some self-defense techniques."

The muscle finally stopped twitching. "Dare I hope he dropped you at home sadder and wiser?"

"Definitely sadder—and sorer. But I don't know about wiser." Especially since his brains were obviously in his balls, which had come out on the losing end with her pointy-toed shoes.

"Probably not. His kind rarely learn." He studied her for a minute.

She twisted her hands together. "And yes, now I know that not all rich guys are like that, but after years of low-level harassment followed up by that one incident, it was too much for me to handle."

Jack nodded. "I understand. But pretend I am not a rich man. How do you feel about me?"

She stared at him, mute with sudden panic.

"Maybe that is not a fair question until you know how I really feel about myself."

A train whistle echoed. Jack gave her a stricken look. "Lily, pass me your train ticket."

"What?"

"Stay to hear me out. Please. Then if you still want to leave, I'll take you to Avignon myself. Or Paris, or wherever you want to go."

She nodded, even though she'd spent practically all her cash on hand on the ticket. But something was telling her to stay as he had asked her. Not ordered, and had even said please. She handed him the ticket and to her surprise he ran away.

He was with Nadine and Lily almost got up then and there to leave, but instead he offered Lily's ticket to the blonde and pointed to the train that was pulling into the station.

Nadine shook her head but Jack jabbed the ticket at her and made several very French, emphatic gestures. She clutched at his T-shirt, but it was so tight she couldn't get a grip. Lily muffled a snicker. That was the type of woman who wouldn't see anything but the exterior. If Jack weren't a doctor, or count or just plain wealthy, Nadine wouldn't be caught dead with a man who wore the T-shirt equivalent of a tube top.

Lily stared at them for any signs of lingering affection and only saw disgust on his face and desperation on Nadine's. She tried to reach up to kiss him on each cheek but he backed away, a deliberate rejection in a culture where people regularly kissed casual acquaintances.

Nadine snatched the ticket from his hand and turned her back on him. The train doors opened and she climbed aboard. Jack, gentleman to the last, handed her luggage after her. Then he came back to Lily, not waiting to see the train depart.

He focused straight on her and the noise of the train and all the passengers receded. "Walk with me, Lily." He took her backpack and pulled her suitcase behind him as they left the station.

"Where are we going?"

"Turn left here." They were in the village square and he chose a seat underneath the giant plane tree. This one was much older than any New World specimens, its low, wide branches reaching fifty feet across and with gently peeling gray paper bark.

"I know how I feel about you, Lily, and this is how I feel about myself." He took a deep breath. "When I was sick in Myanmar, I lost my authority, my dignity, everything. I wasn't Dr. Jacques Montford, Count of Brissard.

I was just another body lying on a cot, unable to move to even care for myself."

"That's horrible." Lily couldn't imagine the conditions he'd been under.

He made an impatient gesture. "It was, but it humbled me. I was used to striding through the camps, stopping to help almost as if I were a Greek god descending from Mt. Olympus to help the mere mortals below."

"Hubris."

"Exactly—overweening arrogance." He shrugged sadly. "But I didn't see it in myself until my outer pretensions were stripped away. I had come to Myanmar to help the people there, but they helped me. Several of them took turns nursing me, giving me spoonfuls of clean water and rehydration salts, changing my bedding, bathing me.

"I had had everything, but I only gave crumbs of myself to them. They had nothing, but they gave everything of themselves to me." He blinked rapidly. "How could I have gone so many years and not seen what a failure I was? What a sham?"

Lily took his hand. "You were not a failure. When you are in a terrible situation trying to help people, you cannot give your whole self away. You'd break down, experience burnout, despair even. You *must* conserve yourself so you can go on to the next disaster in one piece."

"But the arrogance," he protested.

She squeezed his hand. "Stop the presses. Who ever heard of an arrogant doctor? Hey, that reminds me of a great American joke. What's the difference between God and a doctor?"

"What?" he muttered. She could tell he had a good idea of the punch line.

"God doesn't think he's a doctor." Lily raised her eyebrows. "Add to the fact you're a hereditary nobleman whose family has ruled over a large chunk of France for the past thousand years and it's a wonder you haven't tried parting the Mediterranean off the coast of Nice and walking to Corsica."

"Lily!" She'd startled a laugh from him.

"It's true." She plopped her hands on her hips. "I grew up with a lot of rich people who only thought they were nobility, but there was nothing noble about them. I can spot an arrogant phony ten miles away, and you, milord, are about the farthest from being an arrogant phony that there is."

"Then you do care for me."

She still wasn't ready to say it, but she forced herself to anyway. "I guess you could say that because I love you, Jack."

His face lit up. "You do?"

"Yes," she muttered. "That's what made this whole situation so painful. I thought you were this sweet, save-the-world kind of guy, and then you wound up having all this baggage."

Instead of being insulted, he threw back his head and laughed. "Oh, Lily, Lily, only you would call it baggage. That's what I love about you."

She lifted her eyebrow. "That didn't count. What do you love about me?"

"I love *everything* about you," he clarified. "I love how you want to know everything about everybody. I love how you love Provence—the food, the people, the land. I love your writing."

"Are you sure? Because Nadine said—"

He said a bad French word that even she knew. "Forget about her. I love your writing, and I love you."

"Me."

"Of course, you. I fell in love with you as soon as you

bumped into me and asked me about your French accent. Madame Finch knew right away. When we were web chatting with her, she said our meeting was a true *coup de foudre*. Do you remember that?"

She nodded. "What is that—a lightning bolt, or something sudden?"

"It's also slang for love at first sight," he told her, a faint blush staining his cheeks.

She wrapped her arms around his waist. "Oh, Jack, how romantic. I think I fell in love with you when you showed up clean-shaven and promised to act the gentleman with me."

He groaned. "I failed on that part."

"And I'm glad." She tilted her face up and he accepted her invitation, kissing her. Their mouths met as they clung to each other under the shady tree. It was a promise of past, present and future intertwined together.

He finally broke their kiss. "You didn't give me an answer."

"About...?" she answered hazily.

"Marrying me, *ma petite*." He traced his finger down her cheek.

"That? You were just saying that to get my attention."

"No." Jack shook his head. "I meant it then, and now that I am certain you love me, I mean it even more. We can fly back to Philadelphia and marry there so you can have your mother with you. Every bride wants her mother on her wedding day."

"But, but..." she sputtered. "People like you don't get married like that. Don't you have to have a big, fancy wedding with the local bishop and invite every nobleman in Europe?"

"If you met some of those so-called noblemen, you could see why I wouldn't invite them to a flea market.

I will invite my best friends and they will be thrilled to come. And," he added, "your cousin cannot travel for many months now and even until after her baby is born. You need her as your matron of honor."

"Sarah." Lily bit her lip. She had been Sarah's maid of honor and Sarah had vowed to return the favor. "But wait! I haven't even agreed to marry you. And you were already engaged to Nadine. What if this doesn't work out, either?"

"She was the biggest mistake of my life and I thank my lucky stars I found out in time." He dropped to one knee and took Lily's hand. "But you, you are perfect for me. You are brave, honest and true, my Golden Lily. Be my bride. My wife."

She stared down at him, her mind racing. Never in a million years had she expected to find anyone as perfect for her as Jack. "Yes, Jack, I'll marry you."

The joy that burst across his face was contagious, and she started to laugh. He jumped to his feet and pulled her into his arms. "Oh, Lily, sweetheart." He peppered her face with kisses. "I am the happiest man in the world."

"Me, too. I mean…" She laughed again, and he caught her up and twirled her around on the sidewalk.

He set her down. "Lily, would you consider living here in Provence for the next year or so? Jean-Claude and I have several new projects for the farm but he needs my help."

"Hmm." She pretended to think it over. "The south of France year-round? The fabulous food, beautiful views and great weather?"

"It does get chilly in the winter," he warned her.

"Will you keep me warm?" She kissed his neck.

"Sizzling hot," he promised.

"I'll do it." She stood on tiptoes and captured his mouth. "Oh!" She jerked her head back.

"What?" He looked as if he expected her to change her mind. Silly man. It was too late for him to back out now.

"A cookbook! Marthe-Louise and I can do a cookbook."

"Wonderful." Jack smiled down at her. *"Cooking with the Comtesse de Brissard."*

"Good grief. I'm going to be a countess? What about your mother?"

"Sorry. It's automatic when you marry a count. And my mother has been the Dowager Countess de Brissard since my father passed away, so you won't take her title away from her." He wrapped his arm around her shoulder. "I'll introduce you to my friend George's fiancée. It could be worse—she's going to be a crown princess."

"George is a prince? What's Frank, then? A baron?"

"He's a duke."

"Jack!" She elbowed him in the side. "Any more surprises?"

"Only good ones." He kissed the top of her head. "I'll show you the family jewels later."

"I thought you already did." She winked at him and he roared in laughter.

"Ah, Lily, Lily. You are so good for me."

"And you are for me." She snuggled into him. "Take me home, Jack."

"Home to our lavender farm."

"Home to our new life together."

Epilogue

JACK WAVED TO Lily, who was doing lazy laps in the backyard pool at the manor house, and sat down in a chair with his phone.

She swam to the side and rested her elbows on the tile.

"Lily, are we still good for next Saturday?"

"Trying to back out already?" She shook her wet head, darkened to honey by the pool water.

"Never." He would never back out, never give her up.

"Then call your friends. My mother has the chapel booked, and Mrs. Wyndham is hosting the wedding dinner in her house for us."

"As long as your mother and stepfather won't be catering it. They are guests of honor."

"No, they hired their usual outside caterer." She shook her head. "Jack, I can't believe it. Are we crazy for trying to get married in under two weeks?"

He knelt at the edge of the pool and kissed her wet, silky lips. "Crazy in love."

"Good." She swam away, her lithe tan body cutting through the aqua-blue water.

He sat back cross-legged on the pool deck to admire

her for a few seconds and then dialed George first, then got Frank on the line, as well.

After the usual round of greetings and jokes, he came to the purpose of his conversation. "I want you both and Stevie to come to Philadelphia next Saturday."

"Philadelphia? Are we visiting the Liberty Bell?" George asked.

"They do have good cheesesteaks there, George. Mmm," Frank hummed in anticipation.

"Mmm, indeed. Renata, Stevie and I will be in New York, so it would be possible for us, but why should we come to Philadelphia Saturday?"

"Lily and I are getting married," Jack announced proudly.

The brief silence was broken by both his friends offering their warm congratulations. Jack thanked them. "You don't sound very surprised."

Frank laughed. "We knew you were a goner as soon as you told us about her. It was rather entertaining to hear you lose your cool like that."

"Frank," George chided him.

Frank began to hum the melody from "Another One Bites the Dust," and Jack rolled his eyes. "I'm glad my heartache was amusing for you."

"Ignore him," George commanded. "I have a feeling he'll get what's coming to him soon."

Jack laughed as Frank abruptly stopped mid-note. "Frank, come to Philly. You can meet my new countess and get a cheesesteak all in one trip."

"Forget the cheesesteaks. I can't wait to meet Lily," Frank promised. "George, I'll fly into New York and ride down with you and the ladies."

"This won't be our only celebration. Lily and I will have a small ceremony here in the lavender-farm chapel during the harvest festival this fall," Jack explained. "So we can invite all the people here in Provence whom we we care about."

George asked, "But what does your mother say, Jack? I imagine she had a huge wedding planned for one of the big Parisian cathedrals."

"She's coming to Philadelphia, and I promised her a huge reception in Paris this winter during the society season."

"And then Stevie's wedding next June. A wedding for all four seasons." Frank hummed "Here Comes the Bride."

"I'll make sure you catch the bouquet, Frank."

Frank made a choking sound and they all laughed.

"Anyway, guys, come as soon as you can. Lily plans to call Renata to see if she has any ready-to-wear dresses."

"For her, anything," George promised. "Our gift to the bride. If you love her, then she is our family, as well."

Jack swallowed hard. "Thank you."

Frank cleared his throat as if it had tightened, as well. "Give me the address and I'll ship out a case of our best sherry today. We'll drink a toast together in Philadelphia."

"Although we are in three separate countries," George said, "I propose a toast today. To Jack and his bride."

"Hear, hear," cheered Frank. "To a woman as beautiful as her namesake and as patient as a saint to put up with our brother here."

"Hey!" Jack protested halfheartedly. "Well, you're right on both counts."

Lily swam across the pool and smiled invitingly up at him.

"Guys, I have to go now. Lily wants me."

George snorted.

"Ah, the bachelor life passes away with only a whimper," Frank lamented.

Lily floated onto her back and untied her green bikini top, tossing it at his feet. Jack bobbled his phone, catching it before he dropped it into the pool. "Ha! I think married life will be much more fun."

He turned off his phone on the chair and rapidly tossed off his clothes.

She gave him a smoldering glance. "Come on in, Jacky, it's warm and wet."

"I know." He slid into the water. "And so's the pool."

She giggled. "You are so bad."

"You haven't seen anything yet." He found the ties to her bikini bottom and easily removed it.

"DID HE HANG up, George?"

"I believe so, Frank."

"He is a goner, just as I said last week."

"You were right, Frank. And you're next. Renata and I and Jack and Lily will dance at your wedding someday soon."

"Ha!"

"Ha, yourself. I have a feeling, Frank. And you know my maternal grandmother was a fortune-teller."

"Then why can't you ever pick the World Cup winner?"

"Never works for personal gain, old friend."

"Hmmph. Kiss Renata for me."

"I will. *Ciao,* Frank."

"*Ciao,* George."

* * * * *

COMING NEXT MONTH

Available October 25, 2011

You can find more information on upcoming
Harlequin® titles, free excerpts and more at
www.HarlequinInsideRomance.com.

REQUEST YOUR FREE BOOKS!
2 FREE NOVELS PLUS 2 FREE GIFTS!

red-hot reads!

Harlequin® Special Edition® is thrilled to present a new installment in USA TODAY bestselling author RaeAnne Thayne's reader-favorite miniseries,
THE COWBOYS OF COLD CREEK.

Join the excitement as we meet the Bowmans—four siblings who lost their parents but keep family ties alive in Pine Gulch. First up is Trace. Only two things get under this rugged lawman's skin: beautiful women and secrets. And in Rebecca Parsons, he finds both!

Read on for a sneak peek of
CHRISTMAS IN COLD CREEK.
Available November 2011 from Harlequin® Special Edition®.

On impulse, he unfolded himself from the bar stool. "Need a hand?"

"Thank you! I..." She lifted her gaze from the floor to his jeans and then raised her eyes. When she identified him her hazel eyes turned from grateful to unfriendly and cold, as if he'd somehow thrown the broken glasses at her head.

He also thought he saw a glimmer of panic in those interesting depths, which instantly stirred his curiosity like cream swirling through coffee.

"I've got it, Officer. Thank you." Her voice was several degrees colder than the whirl of sleet outside the windows.

Despite her protests, he knelt down beside her and began to pick up shards of broken glass. "No problem. Those trays can be slippery."

This close, he picked up the scent of her, something fresh and flowery that made him think of a mountain meadow on a July afternoon. She had a soft, lush mouth and for one brief, insane moment, he wanted to push aside that stray lock of hair slipping from her ponytail and taste her. Apparently he needed to spend a lot less time working and a great deal *more* time recreating with the opposite sex if he could have sudden random fantasies about a woman he wasn't even inclined to like, pretty or not.

"I'm Trace Bowman. You must be new in town."

She didn't answer immediately and he could almost see the wheels turning in her head. Why the hesitancy? And why that little hint of unease he could see clouding the edge of her gaze? His presence was obviously making her uncomfortable and Trace couldn't help wondering why.

"Yes. We've been here a few weeks."

"Well, I'm just up the road about four lots, in the white house with the cedar shake roof, if you or your daughter need anything." He smiled at her as he picked up the last shard of glass and set it on her tray.

Definitely a story there, he thought as she hurried away. He just might need to dig a little into her background to find out why someone with fine clothes and nice jewelry, and who so obviously didn't have experience as a waitress, would be here slinging hash at The Gulch. Was she running away from someone? A bad marriage?

So…Rebecca Parsons. Not Becky. An intriguing woman. It had been a long time since one of those had crossed his path here in Pine Gulch.

Trace won't rest until he finds out Rebecca's secret, but will he still have that same attraction to her once he does? Find out in CHRISTMAS IN COLD CREEK. Available November 2011 from Harlequin® Special Edition®.

Harlequin Desire

ALWAYS POWERFUL, PASSIONATE AND PROVOCATIVE.

**NEW YORK TIMES AND USA TODAY
BESTSELLING AUTHOR**

BRENDA JACKSON

**PRESENTS A BRAND-NEW TALE
OF SEDUCTION**

TEMPTATION

Millionaire security expert and rancher Zeke Travers always separates emotion from work. Until a case leads him to Sheila Hopkins—and the immediate, scorching heat that leaped between them. Suddenly, Zeke is tempted to break the rules. And it's only a matter of time before he gives in....

Available November wherever books are sold.

brings you
USA TODAY Bestselling Author

Penny Jordan

Part of the new miniseries

RUSSIAN RIVALS

Demidov vs. Androvonov—let the most merciless of men win...

Kiryl Androvonov

The Russian oligarch has one rival: billionaire Vasilii Demidov. Luckily, Vasilii has an Achilles' heel—his younger, overprotected, beautiful half sister, Alena...

Vasilii Demidov

After losing his sister to his bitter rival, Vasilii is far too cynical to ever trust a woman, not even his secretary Laura. Never did she expect to be at the ruthless Russian's mercy....

The rivalry begins in...

THE MOST COVETED PRIZE—November
THE POWER OF VASILII—December

Available wherever
Harlequin Presents® books are sold.

Harlequin®

ROMANTIC
SUSPENSE

CARLA CASSIDY
Cowboy's Triplet Trouble

Jake Johnson, the eldest of his triplet brothers, is stunned when Grace Sinclair turns up on his family's ranch declaring Jake's younger and irresponsible brother as the father of her triplets. When Grace's life is threatened, Jake finds himself fighting a powerful attraction and a need to protect. But as the threats hit closer to home, Jake begins to wonder if someone on the ranch is out to kill Grace....

A brand-new Top Secret Deliveries story!

Available in November wherever books are sold!